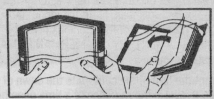

Harlequin Intrigue

REBECCA YORK

Labeled a "true master of intrigue" by *Rave Reviews*, best-selling author Rebecca York makes her Harlequin Intrigue debut with an exciting suspenseful new series.

It looks like a charming old building near the renovated Baltimore waterfront, but inside 43 Light Street lurks danger . . . and romance.

Let Rebecca York introduce you to:

> *Abby Franklin*—a psychologist who risks everything to save a tough adventurer determined to find the truth about his sister's death. . . .
>
> *Jo O'Malley*—a private detective who finds herself matching wits with a serial killer who makes her his next target. . . .
>
> *Laura Roswell*—a lawyer whose inherited share in a development deal lands her in the middle of a murder. And she's the chief suspect. . . .

These are just a few of the occupants of 43 Light Street you'll meet in Harlequin Intrigue's new ongoing series. Don't miss any of the 43 LIGHT STREET books, beginning with #143 LIFE LINE.

And watch for future LIGHT STREET titles, including #155 SHATTERED VOWS (February 1991) and #167 WHISPERS IN THE NIGHT (August 1991).

Coming soon
to an easy chair near you.

FIRST CLASS is Harlequin's armchair travel plan for the incurably romantic. You'll visit a different dreamy destination every month from January through December without ever packing a bag. No jet lag, no expensive air fares and *no* lost luggage. Just First Class Harlequin Romance reading, featuring exotic settings from Tasmania to Thailand, from Egypt to Australia, and more.

FIRST CLASS romantic excursions guaranteed! Start your world tour in January. Look for the special **FIRST CLASS** destination on selected Harlequin Romance titles—there's a new one every month.

NEXT DESTINATION:
THAILAND

 Harlequin Books

JTR2

CHAPTER ONE

FIONA stared down at the contract forms, the words and figures—especially the dollar figures—swimming in her vision. She squinted, trying to focus her sea-green eyes, but it was futile. She might have been looking through rain-washed glass.

Her fingers held the pen like a weapon, her grip so tense that her entire forearm trembled with the strain.

Was she really going to do this? Really going to sink her life savings, her entire future, into ten acres of scrubby land and a house four times older than herself?

Of course she was! She had to, having only minutes before made the final, closing bid at the estate auction in the room next door. The *only* bid!

'Case of last-minute nerves?' The voice of Rob Barron, the estate agent, held only a hint of cynicism; quite clearly he'd seen this reaction many times before.

'A case of too much, too fast,' she replied with a wide grin of her own. 'I know you warned me there mightn't be a lot of interest, but you never suggested I'd be the *only* one bidding.'

'I said you might very well be the only *serious* bidder. And usually there's at least somebody else who'll come in, just to keep the game honest, as it were. And of course I expected to see Dare Fraser here...'

Too late now, she thought, and shivered just a bit inside at her own vindictiveness. Then just as quickly straightened her shoulders against the feeling. Dare Fraser... the name had been hanging over her head like a thunder-cloud ever since she'd first been shown over the property.

Having already fallen in love with the place, she'd been gearing herself up for the disappointment of not being able to afford it and could hardly believe her ears when Rob Barron had named the price he'd expect at auction.

'Unless, of course, Dare Fraser decides he wants it, which wouldn't surprise me. If he gets into the act, there's no telling what might happen,' the estate agent had said.

Fraser... Fiona had—even then—felt a tiny shiver of apprehension. But why? She didn't know the man, had never met him, didn't expect to, and really didn't care. Except, she quickly realised, that if she did buy this property he'd be her neighbour! That only increased her apprehension without providing a single reason why.

'Too late!' This time she whispered the words, and then, keeping the pen well clear of the documents, she worked her fingers experimentally through a practice signature. It was like trying to sign somebody else's name!

Fiona shook her head vigorously, the lengthy, honey-blonde pony-tail swishing behind her. She tried again, this time concentrating even harder, her eyes focused on every twist of the pen.

F-i-o-n-a B-o-y-d; not such a complicated name!

Nor was her signature usually so complicated. Written in the air, in fact, it didn't look like her signature at all.

'This is silly, I know,' she muttered apologetically, hardly daring to meet the estate agent's eyes. He must think her an awful idiot.

'Not silly at all,' he replied. 'You'd be astonished the weird reactions some people have when it becomes time to sign on the dotted line. I had one bloke faint dead away when he sat down just where you are now. And only last week...'

His voice continued, but Fiona no longer caught the individual words. The tone was enough to settle her nerves, to white out the panic that had been writhing inside her like something alive.

Putting pen to paper properly, this time, she scrawled her signature everywhere the estate agent had pencilled in an 'x', then straightened up in her chair and sighed at the quite unexpected trauma involved in all this.

'There we are! Ten per cent down and the rest on the never-never.' She flung down the pen with a sense of physical relief at having the matter done and decided. 'I just hope my dogs appreciate the sacrifice.'

'Oh, I'm sure they will.' Something mildly caustic in the estate agent's tone made her look up sharply, but either he'd hidden it well or she had imagined it. There was only a warm smile now, accepting blandly that anybody would put themselves into hock for years just to please a mob of lazy Labradors.

Fiona was under no true illusion. Her dogs and her lifestyle because of them had played a large part in the decision, but there was more to it than just finding a place where she could raise and train her dogs. There were her own needs to be considered; despite having a bubbly, outgoing personality, she was an essentially private person, and living as she had been in rented accommodation in an inner suburb, with or without three active dogs, was far from her concept of ideal.

There had been only one dog when she'd shifted from Brisbane to Hobart, Tasmania's capital city, nearly four years before. At that time, fresh out of a nasty divorce and glad to have her sanity, her old black bitch and her freedom despite the cost, she'd found the small house she'd rented a relative paradise. Now... well, she'd matured a bit at twenty-five, or at least she hoped so. And she'd saved a good bit of money from her job as a tele-

vision-presenter-cum-weather-girl and the motivational
dog obedience school she'd been operating for the past
year with phenomenal success.

It would take years to rebuild her breeding programme, for which she could thank the ex-husband
who'd managed to cheat her out of several years' work
and even the kennel prefix she'd had since she was
sixteen!

Fiona snarled just at the thought, her mind so buried
in the anger and loathing from the past that she was
hardly aware of Rob Barron's presence. For just that
moment she hated her ex-husband, hated *all* men, every
damned one of them.

Again she shook her head, the pony-tail swishing
viciously. And found the estate agent watching her
nervously.

'I'm sorry,' she said, coldly now and without any real
sense of apology. 'I . . . I was thinking of something . . .'

'Something damned unpleasant, too,' he replied. 'Not,
I hope, to do with our business here.'

'Not in any way that matters.' Fiona shrugged, tried
to force a smile back to her usually mobile features, but
failed. She covered the growing awkwardness by plunging
into her capacious handbag for her cheque-book.

Filling out and signing the cheque for the ten per cent
deposit held none of the trauma of signing the purchase
contracts, possibly because a part of Fiona's mind was
still in what she often thought of as 'active defence
mode'. Before, when her divorce and the bitterness and
treachery of her brief marriage were much fresher, much
more vivid, even frightening, she had learned to set
herself aside, to observe her pain almost as an outsider.
And to conquer it, along with the bitterness and suspicion. Usually.

Today was the first time in months that she'd let the past get to her, and the fact that it was linked to her new start on the future wasn't a good omen, she thought. And snapped back to reality with a tinkle of wild laughter.

'I wonder if I'm not getting superstitious after all,' she said to the estate agent, recalling how she'd denied any such suggestion on her first discovery that the property she wanted had been owned by a woman named Boyd!

'Pure and total coincidence,' she'd said then. 'Has to be, as I don't have any living relatives and I'm not from Tasmania in the first place.'

But she was, now! Fiona had fallen in love with the island state practically in the same move as stepping down from the government-owned Abel Tasman ferry which had brought her and Molly and their battered old Holden utility across from Melbourne—a girl and her favourite dog fleeing the trauma of divorce and betrayal in search of a sanctuary.

With little money, no job and not a single contact or prospect, she had driven southwards from the Devonport ferry terminal, staring at the broad, rugged outline of the Great Western Tiers, and for some reason felt immediately that Tasmania would be a good place for her, a happy, productive place.

After Brisbane, Hobart had seemed small, cosy, comfortable. She'd been fortunate enough to find work at the commercial television station almost immediately, along with a house to rent not far from the channel's headquarters in the inner suburb of Newton.

Fiona's naturally bubbling, apparently open personality had made assimilation easy. She'd quickly made friends, in her own fashion, though nobody was truly close. She wasn't a clothes-horse, nor particularly

interested in the latest fashions or styles, but she was
superbly photogenic and had a gift, quickly appreciated, for working on camera with style and confidence.

Sometimes, she'd thought, it was all because of her
hair. This mass of gently waving, strongly textured mane
was the colour of Tasmania's own bush honey—except
when sun-streaked in summer—and it lent itself to the
type of quick-change restyling so handy in television or
fashion work.

Apart from her hair, which she as often cursed as enjoyed, Fiona had no strong feelings about her looks one
way or the other. She had a good, if not perfect figure,
small breasts, shapely legs, a pretty enough face. And
she was strong and healthy enough for her chosen activities, which was of most importance to her.

And her chosen activities, almost without exception,
involved dogs! Her weekends were spent at dog shows,
dog obedience trials or retrieving trials, her spare time
in preparations and training for them. To her it was perfectly normal that such activities occasionally meant
turning up for work on Monday in a welter of cuts and
bruises—and once a ghastly-looking black eye, courtesy
of her youngest and wildest Labrador. Oh, she sym-
pathised with the station's make-up people, but deep
inside she really couldn't share their fascination with
perfect appearance.

'...say to a celebration drink?' The estate agent's voice
brought Fiona out of her involuntary reverie. 'It isn't,
after all, every day you buy yourself a property, and not
every day that I sell one, though I wish it were so.'

Fiona met his eyes and immediately wished she hadn't.
There was *that* look, the last thing she wanted to see!

'I'd like that,' she lied. 'But not today, I'm afraid. I
had to grovel to get this much time off work, and if I

don't get back soon I'll be trying to pay off this mortgage without even a job.'

The estate agent looked surprisingly disappointed, considering that during their relationship so far he'd never once shown a personal interest like this. Or had he? Fiona had so trained herself out of noticing that maybe he'd been making subtle passes and she'd missed them entirely, she thought ruefully.

But there it was now, for sure. Business completed, Rob Barron had immediately got that too predictable gleam in his eye. Fiona frowned inwardly, then forced a smile. At least he'd waited until the business was done. She knew all too many who wouldn't have.

'I'll call you,' he was saying, but she had already tuned him out—permanently—as she rose and moved quickly towards the door.

Her attention diverted, Fiona didn't notice the murmur of voices in the outer office until she'd already opened the door and stepped through it. And, once through, it was too late to retreat even if she'd wanted to. The murmur clarified to become individual voices, one a growling tide of anger and the other a whining, cringing plea for mercy.

'Fair go, Mr Fraser. I couldn't help it, I tell you . . . I had a flat tyre. It wasn't my fault . . .'

'It won't be your fault, then, when you get the sack!'

The contempt was tangible. Not only in the voice, but in every aspect of the taller, older man's very being. His voice was actually quite soft, though carrying. It was the only soft thing about him.

He loomed over his victim, standing perhaps six feet tall even without the high-heeled stockman's dress boots that gleamed from beneath immaculate moleskin trousers. Large, powerful hands clenched and un-clenched, sending ripples of muscle that even the perfectly cut Harris tweed shooting jacket couldn't totally disguise.

'You were hired to do a job and you've thoroughly stuffed it. You had weeks of notice and weeks to arrange to be here for this auction,' the tall man's voice growled, vibrant with menace. 'If I'd realised how stupidly undependable you are, I'd have come myself in the first place.'

The voice hissed on, vitriolic in criticism of the other, smaller man, but Fiona hardly heard; her mind had focused on that name. Fraser!

Her eyes focused also, taking in every aspect of the tall, angry figure before her. She couldn't see his face, only the sideways angle of strong jawline and the thatch of dark brown hair. Almost impossibly broad shoulders tapered to a narrow waist above the moleskins which could not disguise the well-muscled legs beneath them.

A powerful man, and a man well used to power, she thought. Everything about him cried out in terms of strength, control.

Control? She found herself gasping in horror as one huge hand shot out to seize the smaller man's shirt-front, half lifting him in the tension-charged air.

A squeak of dismay, but it was overshadowed by Fiona's own voice, crackling with anger, projecting with confidence. Her dog-training voice, which had cowed German Shepherds nearly as menacing as this man.

'*Leave it!* You put him down *now*!' The commands snapped out of the background of a thousand obedience rings, a lifetime of retrieving trials, but Fiona was none the less a trifle surprised at how swiftly she was obeyed.

The smaller man was dropped so suddenly that he nearly fell, and Fiona was pinned in her place by dark, piercing eyes that first flashed at her like daggers, then subtly changed as they swiftly traversed every inch of her body before returning to hold her eyes.

'What's your part in this?' The question was in tones so low she barely heard, but there was nothing soft in the visual appraisal he'd made. It had been like being stripped on the auction block, as if her flounce-fronted white blouse and navy office suit hadn't even existed. And the stark arrogance of the man fired her to...speechlessness.

'Well? Are you his mother, or what?' Fraser's dark eyes once again held her own as he loomed above her comparatively diminutive five-foot-three figure.

She visualised herself as a tea kettle, bubbling, burbling and finally boiling over in explosive fury.

'Well, for starters, I'm the owner of the land you so obviously wanted,' she began waspishly. '*I* got here in time, you see.' The last bit she spoke in deliberately contrived sweetness, and she took a token consolation from the flash of fury that told her the blow had been felt.

'Are you, now?' He drawled it out, savouring each word as if it held some special, personal flavour.

'Yes, I am,' she snapped. 'So it's no good your abusing that poor man, because it's too late. Do you understand that? *Too late! Too...*'

Her voice spluttered out helplessly beneath the intensity of his gaze, and suddenly it was as if they were alone in the room, as if Rob Barron, Rob's receptionist, the other man—and was there another woman as well?— had all just been whisked away by some evil magic.

Fiona was conscious now only of this tall, arrogant, menacing figure that seemed to loom above her. She found herself wishing there were some way to chop him off at the knees, so he'd lose that tremendous height advantage, some way to mute the power that flowed from his stance, his voice, from those dark, dark, stone-hard eyes.

She was practically mesmerised. Never had she seen eyes like his; they were ice-cold and hell-hot at the same time, and somehow capable of undressing both body and mind as he surveyed her from crown to high-heeled office shoes, taking in and discarding her navy-blue suit, the pristine white blouse beneath it.

'So you're the lucky bidder...' He seemed to gloat over the words as he whispered them, combining the statement into something neither totally question nor totally accusation.

His voice, like his eyes, touched her. Fiona felt a shudder building at the base of her spine, had to actually straighten herself away from it.

Lucky? With *this* for a neighbour? Fiona again suppressed the shudder. Suddenly the glow of her purchase faded to a dank, gloomy darkness, a darkness matched by the eyes that stared implacably down at her.

She found herself studying the face around those eyes, noting the strong, high-arched brows, the bold, slightly crooked nose, the harsh weather-lines around the eyes. Deep furrows connected his nose to the sides of a broad, mobile mouth, and his chin was deeply cleft.

Not exactly handsome, she found herself thinking, but definitely not pretty, either. He was far too wholly masculine to ever meet that description. Illogically, she found herself wondering what he looked like smiling, and the realisation brought a grin to her own lips.

He didn't return it. One dark eyebrow cocked even higher and his eyes, if possible, became even darker, even more icy, more hard.

'Yes,' she heard herself saying. 'Yes, I'm the buyer, though I'm not sure just how lucky... now.'

Dare Fraser nodded curtly, the gesture seeming to accept both her status and the questionable luck involved.

'So why not take a quick profit and get out of it?' His voice, now so incredibly soft, somehow forced her to listen, to pay attention. But the question, with its obvious lure, was so unexpected that she found herself shaking her head as much in bewilderment as in opposition.

Fraser seemed unperturbed by the reaction. He turned to look at Rob Barron, dismissing Fiona almost as if she no longer mattered, no longer existed, even.

'What was her final bid?'

Barron answered, and although the price could hardly be a secret—it had, after all, been a public auction— Fiona found herself furious at how easily the estate agent appeared to be dominated by this arrogant figure with his overbearing manner.

But Fraser's next remark heaped fuel on the fire, adding insult to insult upon injury.

'Offer her five grand more,' Fraser said, speaking as if Fiona weren't even present. She's only a woman; she doesn't matter, the tone implied.

Fiona couldn't help it. She stamped her foot, slamming the sharp heel into the carpet in confirmation of her long-held belief that this was among the most stupid, futile gestures a woman could ever make.

Now she was not only insulted, but humiliated into the bargain. And she'd done most of it herself! For an instant, she thought of reaching up—far up!—and smacking this insufferable person across the face.

But no, it just wasn't her style. And she definitely would *not* condescend to his level, much as she wanted to force her way into this insane conversation, to assert her rights as a person, as a woman, dammit! Instead,

Fiona took a deep breath, glared once around the suddenly crowded foyer—there *was* another woman there, and Fiona found herself quite astonished at not having noticed her before, because she was amazingly beautiful, elegant in dress and demeanour—then thrust away that impression to turn away from this infuriating Fraser person and march towards the door.

Flinging it open, she was halfway through when something plucked at her collar and she was lifted bodily back into the room with a small squeal of alarm.

'I'm not through with you yet.' Fraser's voice was still soft, but now it held a trickle of amusement that only served to inflame Fiona's temper further.

'I don't personally give a damn what you're through with,' she flared, shaking herself as if simple movement could erase the feel of his hand against her neck.

'Of course you do. This *is* business, after all,' he said with an infuriating calm. 'Or do your Women's Lib tendencies always stand between you and a profit?'

But before she could answer he'd turned again to Rob Barron, who still stood there in the doorway to his private office, his pallid face revealing an almost funny mixture of astonishment and shame.

'Make it six thousand,' said Fraser.

Fiona blew up. How dared this man treat her this way? It was simply intolerable!

'Why don't you make it twenty-six thousand?' she cried. 'Make it a hundred and twenty-six thousand, for all the difference it makes!'

The estate agent just stood there with his mouth open. The smaller man Fraser had been abusing also looked stunned by the proceedings, and even the elegant woman seemed impressed, if one could judge anything by an infinitesimal flicker of one perfect eyebrow. But Fraser only turned to glower down at Fiona; clearly he didn't find anything amusing here.

'Now you're being ridiculous,' he snorted, for the first time in direct speech to her actually raising his voice beyond that strangely gentle whisper.

'Me ridiculous?' Fiona retorted. 'It wasn't *me* who started this. If anybody's being ridiculous, it's you.'

And for the second time she turned away from him, afraid that if she didn't she might give way to that earlier temptation and smack him one.

And just let him put one finger on me again, and I will, too, she thought as she marched towards the door. With every step, she could feel his eyes boring into her back, but then, almost incredulously, that feeling changed as she reached the door and opened it. Now his eyes were blatantly caressing her, reaching out by some magic to touch at the nape of her neck, flutter down the nubbly ribbon of her spine, stroke possessively at the curve of hip...

Fiona shook her head vigorously, her long hair slashing behind her as if that, alone, could dislodge his mental touch. Damn the man, anyway. He was quite mad; he must be!

Suddenly supersensitive, she heard the door swing to behind her, would have known if he'd followed, but he didn't. She turned on to the footpath, a blind left turn that was followed—too late!—by the realisation that her car was to the right. She didn't look back, didn't hesitate, but marched all the way around the block to reach it.

She was late back to work, which nobody noticed, and the pressure of work was such that she got through the remainder of the afternoon with hardly a thought for the arrogant Dare Fraser. It was only when she faced the cameras to do her early evening weather report that he returned to her mind—with a vengeance.

It had always been her practice, when working on camera, to do more than just stare into the coldness of the lens. Like many good presenters, she tended to imagine the audience behind the lens, to give herself and her performance a humanity, a proper link with that invisible audience. Sometimes she visualised one of her dog classes, sometimes a class of schoolchildren, or a theatre audience.

Tonight, like the devil himself, Dare Fraser insinuated himself into the vision, and for the first time in more than a year Fiona blew her lines badly.

Which, of course, *everybody* noticed! Including, she just *knew*, the man himself. He'd have been watching, for sure!

'I don't know what came over me,' she lied once the damage was done, the programme over and done with. 'It must have been just the tension, what with the auction this afternoon and everything.'

'Must have been some auction,' the producer replied with a shake of his head. 'I've never *seen* you blow up like that, even under, well, duress.'

To which Fiona had laughed with delight. Despite whatever the public noticed in famous or infamous television 'bloopers', it was seldom realised how often presenters were deliberately put off their stride by their own colleagues seeking to relieve boredom or stress. Like everyone else, she'd been a victim often enough; unlike everyone else, she had proved herself to be virtually bomb-proof because of an innate ability to improvise. Not that it had helped one bit tonight, she thought angrily.

'Just my luck to be rostered on following an afternoon like that,' she muttered to herself, wondering for the first time if the change to doing weather only on occasional nights instead of regularly five nights a week mightn't be a source of potential problems.

It had better not be, she thought, since the only alternative would be to give up her dog-training school—and that she wouldn't even think about. Since starting the school just over a year before, she had found demand to expand from one evening a week to two, and her dream—still almost too nebulous to dare believe in—was to manage four!

Fiona had done the figures so often she could virtually recite them. Four nights a week, two classes a night, ten students a class and six eight-week terms a year and she might never have to look into a camera lens again!

But it wouldn't be this year, nor probably next year either, not with this mortgage hanging over her head. No, for the time being she'd need to juggle both job and potential career for as long as she could.

She found herself reciting the figures as she drove home, and after greeting and feeding her dogs she curled up with a glass of white wine and her calculator to confirm what she already knew.

'You lot are sending me broke,' she declared, causing the usual differing reactions from each member of the trio that sprawled throughout her lounge-room.

Molly, the oldest, the black foundation bitch of Fiona's current strain, used a subsonic whine to express any and all concerns. It was her worst fault, among several. Being elderly and spoiled was second.

Her daughter Lala, a yellow bitch so pale in colour as to be almost white, became increasingly subservient under pressure or excitement. Her timidity only faded during retrieving trials, when she put on a competitor's façade, and her super-soft, almost Jersey-cow eyes hardened with the joy of competition.

And then there was Trader, the chocolate frog, the bane of Fiona's existence on his *best* days, which were few!

Molly's grandson, and with the same father as Lala, he was impossible to relate to either of them. His mother, also chocolate, had become a private guide-dog for a blind friend and heredity had given her a perfect temperament, intelligence beyond imagining. To her new owner, Magic was quite appropriately named, but while Trader had the family temperament the rest was all his own. Fiona often wondered how she could have bred such a nutcase.

As if she'd spoken to him, the young Labrador bounced to his feet and yodelled as he did his best to wash her face with his tongue. The impetuous action, for whatever reason, served only to remind her of Dare Fraser and his arrogant, thrusting masculinity. There had been one instant that morning when she hadn't been sure if the man had intended to strike her or kiss her, and in retrospect she had to admit she wasn't sure which she'd have preferred.

His sheer physical attraction was beyond question, and although that alone—especially in her working situation—was commonplace enough, Fraser's masculinity had something beyond the usual. It was, she thought to herself, a sort of hard-edged competence. Fraser was a man in touch with himself; he needed none of the vanity and constant reassurance that seemed so much a part of her co-workers in the television industry, where reality itself was little more than just another sort of illusion.

No, Dare Fraser was clearly a case of 'what you see is what you get'. And he didn't care much, Fiona thought, what anyone might think of that.

For the first time, she thought of taking up his autocratic, if ridiculous, offer. Six thousand dollars profit! Ridiculous? It was that and more, but suppose...just suppose...that he might actually be serious?

She had a mental picture of herself dealing with him from a position of power, herself at her most calm and the formerly arrogant Fraser forced to deal on her terms...

Eight thousand? Ten? Twenty? If he was truly rich, and if he truly wanted the place...who could imagine the limits? Fiona spent a whimsical moment exploring ludicrous possibilities along that line, but soon found her thoughts more inclined to her new property and the potential she'd seen for her future there.

She had found the place during one of her 'dog days', times which she often said *normal* people called 'days off'. These were the days supposedly devoted to laundry, housework, a day at the beach, whatever. Not to Fiona! In her mind, an entire day off was far too valuable to waste on simple domestic pursuits, much less lazing about in the sun. She could always find time to wash and iron and dust and shop, especially working the unusual hours she did. But a whole day? That could only mean dogs into the back of the vehicle and off to find a place where they could properly exercise and get some training.

And they knew it! It never mattered how her roster was changed, how little warning might be involved, those dogs knew if it was their day or not. She almost believed they could read other people's minds, because on the rare occasion when she'd been telephoned about a roster change on that very day the dogs had already told her it was going to happen.

The problem with her 'dog days' wasn't the dogs or even their uncanny psychic abilities, but the problem of actually finding a place she could train them without hassles.

First with one dog, then two, and finally the current three, she had driven endless miles, it seemed, fairly covering most of southern Tasmania in search of safe places to run the dogs.

It was a constant exercise in frustration. Problems with stray dogs had made most Tasmanian farmers absolutely paranoid about dogs of any kind. The entire island seemed to be papered with signs proclaiming 'All Dogs Shot'.

Fiona couldn't blame the farmers. All of her own dealings with dogs—and she'd been a professional breeder since she was sixteen and had lived with dogs all her life—put her in total sympathy and agreement with their sentiments.

She knew only too well the problems created by roving packs of strays—usually well-fed city or town dogs knowingly allowed to run at large. She'd seen the slaughtered sheep and other farm animals and had once been saved from possible attack by a feral dog pack only by the intervention of her own companion dogs.

In her dog-training classes, she dwelt heavily on the issues, as did all obedience clubs she knew, but stressing in class the need for responsible dog ownership was of no great benefit in her efforts to find varied but safe places to train, especially for retrieving water work.

The day she'd first noticed the 'Boyd' homestead had been a blustery, drizzly day in late winter. A day sensible, dogless people curled up in front of the fire with a good book.

But of course such people didn't have her trio of emotional blackmailers to stare with soulful eyes, to whinge in either yodels or subsonic whines, to drag out collars, leads, her boots.

'Oh, all right . . . we'll go,' she'd said, and been almost trampled in the rush for the back porch. Minutes later the dogs had been smearing moist noses against the rear windows of Fiona's battered old station-wagon as she crossed the picturesque Tasman Bridge and headed vaguely north.

With hindsight, she realised that she'd passed this particular property without ever noticing it before. Only the 'For Sale' sign with its colourful 'Auction' banner had made the difference this time.

The sign and the open gate had been a magnet to Fiona's curiosity throughout the rest of the morning. She had stood in icy drizzle, freezing while the better-insulated dogs cavorted like mad things, and had absent-mindedly thrown dummies for them over and over again. Then, at the first sign of waning enthusiasm, she had bundled them back into the car and headed homeward, driving carefully in the still poor visibility and keeping an eye out for the signs without being consciously aware she was doing so.

The vehicle, it almost seemed, had turned in of its own accord, steering through the broad avenue of trees— mostly natives—which protected the homestead from the highway. Without the signs and gate, a casual passer-by would hardly have known the house existed.

The house itself was obviously old, low and sprawling in typical Australian country style. But the traditional weatherboards had been painted regularly, from the look of it, and overall it seemed in fair condition.

The gardens were now neglected, but only recently so, from their appearance, and at their best must have been truly marvellous. Otherwise, well . . . there were various outbuildings in equally various states of disrepair. A weary but solid old barn, a couple of questionable dog runs and a chicken run with movable fencing to give the chickens an occasional change of scratch, and the remains of a substantial kitchen garden.

Fiona had looked through the steamy car window for several moments, then stepped out into the streaming rain for a closer look. The house, logically enough, was locked, but the shelter of the spreading verandas gave her time to peer into every window and get a remarkably accurate picture of the layout.

It was smaller than she'd originally thought, or else it just appeared that way because the rooms were fairly large, she ultimately decided. But surely there were only two bedrooms—each with its own fireplace, no less!— a huge, empty lounge-room with a built-in, modern wood-heater inside the fireplace, and an equally enormous and apparently well-appointed kitchen that looked workable if not exactly ultra-modern.

The kennels, by comparison, were dreadful.

Sagging wire partitions and very questionable gates made the chicken run a safer proposition from a security point of view. Fiona hadn't dared to examine the barn; that could wait for a proper, legal visit with the estate agent.

She'd been forced to guess direction, and later found that the house had been positioned—as she'd guessed— just right to catch the maximum winter sun in the living areas. But even in the rain, with low cloud scudding the distant hills, the place had *something*. Before she'd properly seen the inside, before she'd even heard of that unknown, earlier Miss Boyd, Fiona had been smitten.

What was more, she'd stayed that way, albeit with many reservations, during the visits she'd later made with the estate agent. The more she'd seen of it, the more she'd seen of problems that wanted fixing, of things that needed paint or paint removing or repairs, the more she'd loved it all.

She had attended each of the pre-auction open days, growing increasingly restive as hordes of Nosy Parkers had tramped through the house, voices raised in criticism of this aspect or that, their attitudes so boorish they had made her froth with anger.

'They're animals, most of them,' she complained to Rob Barron; they were becoming almost conspirators at this stage, she had felt.

He'd merely laughed. Although in sympathy with Fiona's feelings, he'd seen this all before. Still, he had offered some slight consoling.

'You won't see any of them at the auction—or at least not with money in their pockets,' he'd said. 'Sure, some will come for a look, but I haven't seen a fair-dinkum buyer yet, bar you.'

'And this Fraser person,' she had replied, even then feeling that inexplicable hostility which the very name of Fraser seemed to produce. Now, of course, she knew why!

It was ridiculous, but she knew she had been, if only subconsciously, watching everyone who prowled through the house—*her* house, she couldn't help thinking—and wondering which of these intruders might be that man Fraser, but he had never come.

'You might get lucky. He might be land poor just at the moment, or have other places to put his money,' Barron had said, seeming mildly amused by her unspoken concern. 'But don't get your hopes too high, just in case. Fraser knows this place; it used to be part of what's now his property. And if he decides he wants it, he can afford to outbid you or anybody else who might be interested, I reckon.'

So during the final weeks, weeks that were a constant merry-go-round of banks and lawyers and more banks, all of it had been tinged with the unseen shadow of a man she'd never met and wouldn't know if she did meet him. But now, she had!

Fiona stopped her pacing with a sudden, exultant laugh. She rushed to refill her wine glass and raised it triumphantly.

'And to hell with you, Dare Fraser,' she cried! 'Too late!'

CHAPTER TWO

'YOU really should have taken the money and run while you had the chance, but then I suppose you know that.'

'Oh, yes, but of course I didn't think of that at the time, did I?' Fiona replied with a cheeky grin. She quite liked her lawyer, who'd been a friend almost since her arrival in Hobart. He was a tall, almost cadaverously lanky individual with the driest sense of humour she had ever encountered.

'Well, you should have; a six-thousand-dollar profit for five minutes' work isn't to be sneezed at, or in your case more probably growled at.'

'Growled is exactly right. The man just made me so damned angry...'

'All the more reason to have taken his money. What kind of a neighbour do you expect him to make now? You've refused a perfectly good offer, growled at him into the bargain, and now you're about to add insult to injury by moving in before he has any chance to repeat the offer or negotiate at all.'

'But, John, that's why I bought the place—to live there. I didn't buy it to resell to Dare Fraser or anyone else.'

'With six thousand dollars extra, you could have bought a place handier to town and with the chance of less hostile neighbours. It does bear thinking about, even now.'

'Not to me!'

The lawyer scowled, but Fiona could tell he wasn't all that angry. 'I suppose you've not talked to your estate

27

agent since this performance either?' he asked then. 'For all you know, this Fraser might have come up with a real live offer.'

'If he had, I'm sure Mr Barron would have tried to reach me with it. After all, think of the double commission he'd be getting for doing almost nothing at all. No, I think Fraser was talking through his hat, or just so angry at the time that he decided to try me on. But I don't think he was all that serious.'

The lawyer's scowl now *was* serious. 'I think you may find there's more to Dare Fraser than you reckon,' he said. 'He's got a fairly hefty reputation for getting what he wants.'

'So have I,' Fiona replied grimly. 'And I want *my* property, which I have paid for. If Dare Fraser doesn't like it he can just damned well put up with it.'

'Or you'll set your dogs on him, I suppose. Speaking of which, how's the horrible one now that he's been fixed?'

Fiona laughed. 'He'll never be the dog his father is, but I suspect if he lives long enough he'll settle into something fairly useful.' Trader's father was, in fact, a yellow dog she'd arranged for John to get several years earlier, and he, too, had now been 'fixed', in his case to cure him of endless love-lorn roamings. 'I presume Murphy's a bit better behaved now?'

'Infinitely,' was the pleased response.

Having finalised settlement of the purchase, Fiona spent the next few days organising to have the electricity reconnected, and the telephone. Water was her own problem, coming as it did from the large rainwater tanks beneath the spreading eaves of the old house.

The tasks were more difficult than she had expected, as was arranging the movement of her small supply of furniture and buying the various essentials she now required. Her former house had been rented fully furnished; now she had empty rooms to fill and nothing to fill them with. Not even, for the first few days, a proper bed.

But by the following weekend she was essentially settled in and generally pleased with the results of much scrubbing and dusting.

The biggest problem, she found, was the totally inadequate kennels. With Lala coming into season, there was an immediate need to create a secure kennel block, so on this Saturday morning Fiona found herself returning from Hobart with her station-wagon labouring under a load of weldmesh fencing panels.

She was approaching her driveway when the police patrol car wheeled up behind her, roof lights flashing. It wasn't until she got out of the vehicle that she realised one of the fencing panels was dangling dangerously off the roof-rack.

'A bit dangerous, lady,' said the policeman, stepping from his vehicle with an aura of brisk authority.

'I'm really sorry,' Fiona replied, flushed with embarrassment. 'I didn't realise...'

'You'd have realised quick enough if some of that lot had fallen off into the road in front of somebody driving behind you,' the policeman replied sternly, then ignored her as he stalked around her old station-wagon, observing every detail of vehicle and load with a jaundiced eye.

She had already fished through her handbag for the driving licence she expected him to ask for, but the question was forestalled by the arrival of yet another observer—one whom Fiona would have gladly taken the expected ticket just to avoid.

Fiona watched in her rear-vision mirror, the policeman standing silent beside her, as the unmistakable figure of Dare Fraser unfolded itself from the cabin of the farm utility vehicle and approached.

Was there, she wondered, a distinct gleam of satisfaction in those dark eyes? Very likely! She could just imagine how pleased this man must be at her predicament.

And now what? Would he join the policeman in giving her a well-deserved ticking off? Or perhaps use his local influence to ensure a heavier than normal penalty? She had a momentary flash of *déjà vu*, could almost hear Fraser's cryptic, scathing description of the incident when he appeared in court as a witness to her carelessness.

But his first words, to her great surprise, were anything but scathing!

'Bit of bad luck with that lashing,' he commented with a quick look at the problem. Nothing in his manner revealed the joy Fiona knew he must be feeling.

'Very dangerous situation, sir,' said the policeman, and Fiona found herself distinctly miffed at the respect which Fraser so easily commanded.

'Indeed. And very fortunate, I'd say, that you were on hand to alert Miss Boyd to the danger,' Fraser replied smoothly. The smile he gave the policeman was genuine enough, but Fiona noticed how easily it created a man-to-man atmosphere from which she was automatically excluded.

Neither man so much as glanced at Fiona as they strolled round the vehicle, discussing the problem as some merely academic exercise in the carrying of bulky, unwieldy materials.

Fiona could only follow in their wake, becoming increasingly embarrassed as the foolishness of her situation was discussed.

The gates and steel posts for her new kennel had fitted inside the station-wagon without difficulty, but the sheer size of the eight-foot-by-two-metre panels had forced her to try to carry them on the roof. It was that, or have them delivered, which would have meant a weekend wasted while she waited for the Monday delivery. By carrying them herself, she could start work on the structure immediately, so she'd taken the chance.

At the time it had seemed a reasonable enough decision, but as she viewed the precarious load through the men's far more experienced eyes she realised how criminally stupid she'd been.

The weight of the panels had forced the entire roof-rack out of alignment, and her inexpert attempts to lash the dozen panels in place had only compounded the problem.

I'm lucky the whole issue didn't spill into the road on the very first curve, she thought, and cringed when Dare Fraser voiced almost identical thoughts to the nodding agreement of the policeman.

But her cringe turned to outright astonishment at her neighbour's next remark. Astonishment followed by total bewilderment and disbelief.

'I suppose I'll have to take most of the blame,' she heard Fraser say, and looked up to find him glaring at her as if to stifle any challenge. 'If I hadn't been so late, Miss Boyd wouldn't have been forced to try such a risky undertaking. We're neighbours, you see, and I was supposed to get there on time to bring this stuff back in the ute.'

The blatancy of the lie was too much for Fiona, who stood there—speechless—as Fraser steered faultlessly through a complicated explanation about why he'd been late, and how she must have presumed he wasn't coming after all.

It was, she determined, a masterful exercise in deceit; the policeman listened patiently to every word and was clearly taken in by the lies.

Throughout the telling, Dare Fraser shot commanding glances in her direction, and the message was unmistakable—not one word! Fiona stewed, confused by Fraser's gambit, but she obeyed.

When Fraser had finished, he gave Fiona no chance to get in an explanation of her own. With hardly a glance in her direction, he disentangled her lashings and started switching the weldmesh panels into the back of his utility vehicle.

Just for an instant, she thought the policeman was going to be conned into helping, but a yelp from the police radio in the patrol car diverted his attention, and after a muttered conversation he waved to Dare Fraser and drove away.

'You might give me a hand with this, seeing as I'm late already.' Fraser's voice was no longer congenial as it had been with the policeman. Now it grated, and as Fiona turned to face him she could see that his story hadn't been the only deceitful thing about the man. His gaze was cold, his manner brusque, almost angry.

She rushed to help, despite an immediate wish that he'd left the panels alone. This close to home, she could have managed on her own, but now that he'd shifted more than half of them she couldn't reasonably refuse his assistance.

'I'm really very grateful for this,' she began, reaching to grip her end of the next panel as he lifted it from the top of the vehicle.

Fraser merely growled.

'You ought to be grateful you didn't kill somebody with this stuff,' he said. 'Preferably whoever taught you ver occur to you to stop and check,

d, scooting to keep up with his
ed her along with him towards

ne more so because she knew he was
bit her tongue to keep from a testy reply
ignored her and continued his harangue.

hy the hell you didn't have it delivered in the first
ace, I can't imagine,' he said.

'They couldn't deliver it until Monday, and I'd have
wasted the entire weekend waiting for it,' she replied,
careful to keep her own voice reasonable, conciliatory.
'And besides, they charge for delivery and I'm on a very
tight budget.'

Inwardly, she was starting to fume. Bad enough he
had to get involved, but just because he'd saved her a
traffic ticket there was no reason to think he could start
running her life for her.

'So instead of a small delivery fee, you're going to
cop mighty penalty rates getting somebody to work on
the weekend,' he replied with a sneer, gesturing at her
to grab her end of the next panel.

Fiona was hard put to it to match his pace, and her
reply was gasped out.

'I'm going . . . to do it . . . myself,' she panted, trotting
to keep up as he marched again to his utility vehicle.

Fraser said nothing until they'd laid the fencing panel
on top of the others. Then he straightened and stared
down at Fiona, seeming to see her for the first time.

She met his gaze squarely, suddenly conscious of her
faded, ragged blue jeans and scuffed running shoes, the
fact that her jumper was stained and her make-up non-
existent.

Dare Fraser, by comparison, was almost in
His moleskin trousers were clean, showing th
of recent ironing. His own jumper was tidy
checked shirt and even his elastic-sided boots
spotless.

He was freshly shaven, and the dark hair that flopp
down across his forehead was clean and only slight
mussed by the breeze. Once again, Fiona found hersel
seeking a better word than handsome, a more appropriate word to portray the sheer power of the man.

He loomed above her, seeming taller than the six-foot
height she reckoned. And his eyes, black with anger only
moments before, now flashed with amusement. Or
contempt!

One dark eyebrow cocked, he allowed a flicker of a
smile to cross that mobile mouth, then turned away and
marched back to heave at another fencing panel, glancing
down into the back of her station-wagon as he approached it.

Clearly visible inside were the gates, the posts and the
various bits and pieces required for erecting the fencing,
along with a rented post-hole digger.

As Fiona rushed forward to take up her end, Fraser
waved her away disdainfully. 'You'd best save your
strength,' he muttered, easily lifting two panels together
above his head and carting them across to the other
vehicle.

'Hang on,' she cried, angry now at the implied slur
as well as at being so abruptly dismissed. She trotted
after him, only to find herself forced to step aside as he
loaded the panels and turned quickly to return for the
final pair.

Fraser merely looked at her briefly before picking up
the panels and returning to his utility vehicle with them.

'Don't forget your ropes,' he said. 'You might need them to hold all this together.'

And before she could reply he had turned away to get into the cab, where he sat, drumming his fingers on the steering-wheel and obviously waiting for her to take the lead.

Fiona returned to start her own vehicle, fairly shaking with anger as she—after carefully checking for on-coming traffic—pulled on to the highway for the brief journey home.

Damn the man and his arrogance, she thought. Just because of one slipped knot, he was going to treat her like a total incompetent. Worse, he would get away with it, now that he'd so handily put her in a position of being obliged to him.

Fraser followed as she drove into the yard, but was curiously incurious as he offloaded the weldmesh panels and stacked them against the side of the barn.

Fiona found it unusual that he showed no apparent interest in either the house or the outbuildings, asked no questions about her plans, her reasons for having bought the property, or anything else.

Her own anger at his attitude had fled; vindictiveness was not strong in her. And once the work was done, she was faced with putting a polite face on the whole ordeal.

'Thank you for everything,' she said. And then, 'Would you like a drink, or coffee or something?'

Fraser glanced down at his now grimy hands and re-plied, 'I wouldn't knock back the chance to clean up; I've an appointment in the city.'

'And you're already late. I'd forgotten that,' she said, grateful for the fact despite feeling mildly guilty. Dare Fraser seemed to dominate his surroundings far too much for her taste, and while politeness was obviously re-quired she wouldn't be unhappy to see him go.

'It's no great hassle,' he replied unexpectedly. 'And, if you'll show me where I can wash, I'd love a cup of coffee.'

She led him to the back door and—without thinking—opened it to an explosion of dogs that very nearly knocked her over in their excitement. Then they realised she wasn't alone, and Dare Fraser was treated to a concert of raised hackles and suspicious barks and growls.

'That'll do!' she cried, only to be ignored by all three as they swarmed around Fraser's feet.

Her guest seemed also to ignore her. He stood stock-still, since to move without kicking or treading on a dog would have been impossible.

But it wasn't through fear or apprehension; even as Fiona watched, he slowly descended to a semi-crouch, emitting an almost soundless whistling as he did so and letting those huge, muscular hands rest across his knees with knuckles outstretched to the pack around him.

The effect was magical; the cacophony of growls and yodels halted immediately as the dogs thronged forward to sniff at Fraser's hands and trouser legs. He stayed in position until each dog had made its inspection, then slowly rose to his full height and growled, 'Sit!'

Which, to Fiona's astonishment, they did. Even the incorrigible Trader plunked his bottom down in recognition of this undeniable higher authority.

'Good dogs,' Fraser announced in recognition, and then stepped past the animals and into the house, Fiona trailing in his wake as the dogs sat quietly and watched.

'I won't be a minute,' he said, striding off towards the bathroom, and it wasn't until he was out of sight down the corridor that she realised that, although he had earlier mentioned being shown where to wash, he had needed no showing at all. He knew *exactly* where things were in this house.

That, for some reason, bothered her not at all. It was almost as if she'd expected such familiarity, somehow!

Fiona had the electric jug boiling when he returned, but she found the polite routine of serving coffee, asking if he took milk, sugar, getting the expected responses, frustrating in the extreme. She didn't care how he took his coffee—she wanted to know how he knew so much about the inside of *her* house!

Worse, the devil knew how she felt. Each glance of those observant dark eyes around the kitchen told her he was making some assessment of her so-far minuscule changes to the way the kitchen had been.

And he was so quiet. Instead of filling the silences with idle conversation, he merely sipped at his coffee, glancing occasionally round the room, occasionally at her. Silent, assessing, somehow vaguely threatening.

And when he finally did speak, it wasn't about the house, wasn't about her own curiosity.

'You'll need a crowbar to get those posts in the ground here,' he said without preamble. 'There's a helluva lot of rocks.'

Having no idea what he was talking about, she could only nod an acceptance when he continued by saying he happened to have one in the truck and would leave it with her.

Moments later he was rising to leave, having recognised her curiosity and chosen—deliberately, perhaps even maliciously, she realised—to ignore it. He *knew* this house and, worse, he knew that she recognised that fact, knew she wanted information. And wasn't going to give it to her.

The dogs greeted them with an unexpectedly subdued attitude when they returned to the yard, almost as if they had already accepted Dare Fraser's mastery. It was an attitude Fiona found infuriating; they should be threatening to have the man's left leg for lunch, she thought angrily, not kowtowing to him as if he were some minor god!

Even more infuriating was the ease with which he hefted an enormous iron fencing crowbar from the bed of his utility vehicle and handed it to Fiona as if it were a twig. The weight of the mighty bar, which had a round knob at one end and a sharp wedge at the other, staggered her to the point where she almost dropped the tool, which was almost as tall as herself.

'I shouldn't need this for a day or two,' he said with a wry smile at her discomfiture. 'Will that be long enough for you?'

'I would expect so,' she lied, afraid to admit that she hadn't the faintest idea how long it might take her to sink the posts that would hold the fencing panels in place. She felt stupid, now, about even attempting the construction herself. She had seen plenty of kennels built, had even helped in such projects to a minor degree, but it had been financial pressures, not experience, that had forced her into this particular project.

Dare Fraser shrugged. 'Well, you want to be surer than that before you order the concrete,' he said, again with that horrid, wry smile.

Fiona blanched. 'What concrete?' she asked. 'I'd just planned to fence in a decent run, for now, and worry about concreting later.' A subtle way of saying she couldn't afford to concrete the floors of the runs; her budget was blowing out all logic as it was. 'None of my dogs is a digger, so it should be all right. And besides, I want to keep a section of the centre in grass, especially around that tree.'

She had mentally planned the run to encircle an enormous cotoneaster at the edge of the back garden. This large spreading shrub with its winter berries would give the dogs year-round shade during the hot part of the day, yet could be pruned to allow morning and evening sun to penetrate.

Fraser smiled again, this time a self-satisfied, almost smug grin.

'I don't fancy your chances of getting away with it,' he said. 'Ever since this new state dog act went through, the council's been getting more and more sticky about what constitutes "proper" kennels.'

Then he shrugged, as if to say it wasn't *really* all that important, and added casually, 'You might get lucky and get your kennel licence without an inspection, provided there aren't any objections, of course.'

A shiver of warning shot through her, so vivid that Fiona imagined even Fraser could see it. The kennel licence! She had totally forgotten about that, despite having thoroughly boned up on the new dog act when it came out.

It was a horribly complicated piece of legislation, the upshot of which was that any person keeping more than two dogs *must* have a kennel licence, and that licence depended upon specifics governing the type of kennel facility, the closeness of neighbours, and a variety of other things.

One of which was the objections of any neighbour closer than two hundred metres! And, since Fraser had mentioned it, there was every reason to believe he might intend using the act against her.

Then logic took over. The two-hundred-metre clause might well take the issue beyond her own boundaries and on to his, as well as that of her other neighbour, but neither property's buildings or homestead were anywhere near within that distance. Surely she could have no problems with the council on that score!

But on the subject of just exactly how kennels must be constructed... well, she'd have to look into that. But not until Fraser was gone. She didn't dare give him the satisfaction of realising how much his apparently casual comments had shaken her, because his mention of the dog act had spurred other clauses to mind, especially those involving any farmer's right to shoot any stray dog on his property, regardless of whether it might be harassing stock.

Almost as if he had read her mind, Fraser was allowing his gaze to run along the boundary fences that separated their two properties.

'I might get somebody down to check out that boundary fence, too,' he mused, almost as if he were talking to himself. 'Unless you're sure your dogs aren't jumpers, either?'

'They aren't,' she replied, her voice peevish as she perceived the potential threats involved in this discussion. 'Not that it would matter, since they're thoroughly bomb-proof where stock is concerned. I could take any of them through the middle of your lambing paddocks—off lead—and never have to worry a bit.'

Fraser's smile now was grim. 'It wouldn't be then that I'd worry about them,' he said, voice soft now, but deadly. 'It's when you're *not* with them that I'm concerned about.'

'When I'm not with them, they're at home where they belong,' Fiona replied stoutly, forcing herself to meet his stern gaze. Essentially, that was the absolute truth, but she knew only too well that, with dogs, there was always the exception, always the accident that resulted in a gate being left open, always at least the *chance* that a dog could get loose, could chase stock, could . . .

A mental picture flashed up of an acquaintance who lived on a farm near Broadmarsh with two big German shorthaired pointers. Walking the dogs on her own property one Sunday, the woman hadn't been overly concerned when one went missing, until the dog had returned ten minutes later with blood all over its muzzle and she had found herself having to face an irate neighbour with a slaughtered goat.

That little incident, Fiona recalled, had meant reparation of a hundred dollars—for a scrubber of a goat that probably hadn't been worth five dollars. But the money had saved the dog's life, until he had done it again several months later and had to be put down for the sake of peace in the neighbourhood.

Even her own Molly, in the final week of pregnancy, had been known to go walkabout, instinctively seeking to lay up a good food store to carry her through the early days of whelping. But she'd never touched stock!

Fiona sighed, hardly aware at that instant of Fraser's presence. She would *have* to see to concreting at least the edges of her runs, would *have* to find the money somewhere.

She shivered inwardly again, unwilling to face the power this man now had over her. Let one dog cross that boundary, sheep-chasing or not, and he could shoot it with the full authority of the law. Let her not build her new runs to the exact specifics of the dog act, and he could intervene to force her, could object to her *ever* getting a kennel licence.

Just for an instant, the enormity of the situation came near to defeating her. Her shoulders slumped and she stared at the expensive kennel fencing panels, the weekend's work ahead of her, and felt like chucking it all in.

Let him have the property if he wanted it, because he'd probably end up getting it anyway.

But only for an instant. Then defiance set in, along with an anger at the unfairness of it all.

'I'm keeping you from your appointment,' she reminded him, hoping against hope that he'd take the hint and just *go*!

She had all this work ahead of her, all these Fraser-induced worries now to sort out, and the horrid man just stayed there, his gaze roving over *her* property with a too proprietorial eye.

'I'm already late; a bit later can't matter,' he said with supreme indifference. It was the type of indifference that suggested the man's knowledge of his own situation, the knowledge that if he were late *whoever* was waiting would wait, would have to wait.

Supreme indifference, Fiona thought, and supreme arrogance with it. Couldn't he take the hint, couldn't be see that he wasn't wanted here, despite his earlier help?

Now he was looking at the large, spreading shrub, then over at the stack of fencing panels, clearly calculating something in his mind.

'Good idea to incorporate the tree,' he mused, 'although you may regret it during the berry season when the place is swarming with mountain parrots. Still...' And without a word of further consultation he was striding off to roughly pace out boundaries for the new kennel block.

Fiona could only watch; he clearly wasn't going to *consult* her. So she watched... and fumed.

'What are you going to use for the shelter?' he asked suddenly. 'Separate dog houses or...'

'I haven't got that far yet,' she lied. In truth, she'd thought it out quite carefully. An acquaintance had evolved a splendid set-up using a children's playhouse made from treated pine planking. For Fiona's situation it had great possibilities, being high enough for her to move around inside, easy to clean, and not all that expensive in the long term. For the moment, such a structure would be perfect, though she'd have to have two separate facilities if she decided to get back into breeding.

'Two runs, then, or just one?' Dare Fraser hadn't noticed the lie, or wasn't interested. He was planning this all in his mind, doing *her* planning, Fiona thought half angrily.

'How about three?' she replied sarcastically. 'There are three dogs, after all.'

This time, he noticed. One dark eyebrow lifted in steely acknowledgement of her foul temper, but he merely quirked his lip in what might have been a smile.

'Three damned small runs if these are all the panels you can afford,' he replied finally, eyes turning as he counted the panels once again. 'Two, I think, with a common run around the cotoneaster.'

And, taking the heavy fencing bar from her suddenly nerveless fingers, he began using the sharp end to trace a plan for the project on the ground around the shrub, speaking—either to her or to himself—as he did so.

Fiona could only listen, fascinated despite her frustration at the way he was taking over.

'The prevailing wind's here,' he said, pointing the huge bar as if it weighed nothing, 'so you'll want your shelter block at this end, facing that way. Easier to bring in the power and water there, too, when you're ready. And if we manipulate the shape...this way...you'll end up with a good, sheltered sun-trap for winter.'

It was incredible. Where she had envisaged square or rectangular shapes, given the consistent sizes of the fencing panels, Fraser had plotted a far more useful system that took into account every advantage of the site.

'But that's brilliant!' she cried, frustration forgotten as she saw the excellence of his plan. 'It's absolutely perfect; there's even a place I can expand with a puppy run when it's time. But how did you figure it out so easily?'

Fraser's grin, genuine now as he shared her pleasure, was none the less modest. 'Not real difficult,' he said quietly. 'I'm an architect, though I don't work at it full time.'

'It's wonderful,' she smiled. 'I can't thank you enough, honestly.'

Then she paused, caught by some glimmer behind those dark eyes, suddenly made cautious by the memory that this man wanted her land, the knowledge that despite his help today he was still very much a potential threat.

But as quickly as she noticed it, the look was gone. And so, a moment later, was Fraser. He handed her the heavy fencing bar, quietly said, 'See how you get on,' then stepped into his truck and drove off without even a wave.

His was a strange, almost contradictory attitude, Fiona thought several times during an afternoon of the hardest physical work she'd ever done in her young life.

He should, she thought, resent her being here. He did! And yet, he'd not only helped her, but had actually *lied* for her. She couldn't figure that out, and no amount of sparring with the contradiction seemed to help.

She could understand, however, why he'd grinned so easily when mentioning the rocks. Beneath the shallow topsoil, it seemed, the property was little more than a gigantic gravel pit!

Fraser had only been gone ten minutes when she'd discovered the hard work that lay ahead of her. The rented post-hole digger—as he had known, she muttered ruefully to herself—was worse than useless in the stony soil. Every single post hole she dug had to be dug inch by inch, using the heavy fencing bar to break up the stony soil, to pry loose the endless layers of loose rock and shale that lay beneath the soil.

There wasn't even room to use a shovel—not that she had one. By teatime her fingers were gouged and cut and filthy, her nails broken and the knees worn out of her jeans from kneeling on the stony ground.

And her temper? Fiona had used up every curse she knew and was finding an incredible ability to think up new ones with every piece of jagged stone she dragged from the growing line of post holes.

Her acknowledgement of Fraser's planning brilliance was undiminished, but to it had been added a quite illogical anger when she had—after laboriously digging the first hole—decided it might be sensible to *measure* his rough plan before she went any further.

And finding that his calculations and measurements—done by eye alone—were never more than one inch out somehow only served to make her temperament worse instead of better.

Especially, she realised, since without his guidance she'd have made an unholy botch-up of the entire project, would indeed still be planning and measuring, instead of having half the poles already in place.

'Thank you, Mr Fraser, I think,' she sighed, stretching and arching her back to try and relieve a growing ache that would be worse—far worse—by tomorrow.

The dogs were no help at all. When they weren't getting in her way, trying to establish this peculiar activity as some new kind of game, they were asleep under the cotoneaster bush, rousing only to the loudest of her curses.

By dark, she could hardly stand, her back hurt so much. And her hands, Fiona reckoned, had been permanently curled into claws from the effort of wielding the heavy fencing bar. She managed to summon just enough energy to feed the dogs, throw herself under the briefest of showers, and stagger into bed, exhausted.

The Sunday was sheer torture, and Dare Fraser's arrival just before lunchtime did nothing to help!

Fiona, struggling to straighten, to get up from her knees as the dogs went mad and rushed the gate, kicking half her hard-won gravel back into the current post hole as they passed, only just managed to stand as Dare Fraser stepped from his truck and approached her.

His eyes flashed over her exhausted body, noting the kneeless jeans—she wasn't going to ruin *two* pairs—the smudges of dirt, the now thoroughly blistered hands with their ruined nails, the carelessly bound hair.

And the look in her eyes, which was enough to diminish his grin considerably. Though not entirely. As Fiona steadied herself with the hated fencing bar, knowing she was swaying slightly and too exhausted to care, he cast a knowing eye around the site.

I don't need this, she thought as he stalked around the perimeter, inspecting each individual post, seeming to check on her measurements, on whether each post was perfectly upright, exactly the right depth. Only then did his eyes return to Fiona herself, and now the smile was gone.

'You're a glutton for punishment, I'll give you that,' he said in that too soft voice.

Fiona wasn't sure if that was a compliment or not. And didn't care. She didn't need him here, didn't want him here. This was *her* land, *her* project. And he'd interfered enough. Probably an unfair attitude on her part, but just now she didn't care. All she wanted to do was get finished, to have this torment over with.

'What do you want?' she asked brusquely, knowing she must sound rude, *was* rude, but not caring.

Fraser's eyes narrowed slightly, but his voice showed none of the offence he should have felt.

'Just thought I'd see how you were getting on,' he said quietly. And gestured to his truck, piled high with fencing wire. 'I'm on my way to remake that boundary fence,' he added, pointing towards the fence-line that separated their two properties.

'And just stopped to gloat, I suppose,' Fiona snarled, knowing she was being unreasonable, unable to stop herself. Throughout the day she'd found herself wondering about this man, trying to justify his change—apparent change—of attitude.

She couldn't. It was as simple as that. The deep-seated resentments left over from her marriage, from the betrayals involved with it, had boiled up from somewhere to leave her incapable of accepting his interest, his help, without deep suspicion. He must have an ulterior motive, and in her present condition she was in no shape to evaluate anything, much less protect herself against it.

Dare Fraser was silent for a moment, his eyes gone cold as he felt her rudeness. His stare was chilling, devoid of any emotion. Fiona had seen that kind of stare before, in the blank, beer-bottle eyes of a kelpie just before it had attacked her. Now, irrationally, she steeled herself for a similar attack, but in vain.

'If you say so,' he replied finally, and before she could reply he had turned on his heel and was moving swiftly towards his utility vehicle, only the rigidness of his bearing giving evidence of the anger she knew must be there.

She started to say something, to explain, to apologise...*anything*, but it was too late. She sagged against the rigid strength of the fencing bar, dogs at her feet, as he quickly reversed the vehicle and was gone.

Fiona felt a fool, having realised instantly just how rude and silly she'd been. There was no satisfaction in it, and less in the fact that throughout the afternoon, every time she looked up from her labours, she could see the tall, rangy figure of her neighbour in the distance.

He finished his fencing work before she did, although not by much, and worse, he did it without once acknowledging her presence, without once appearing to notice when her dogs barked at his distant figure.

When she straightened up for the final time, just before four o'clock, he was gone, leaving in his wake a run of new, shiny netting fence along one entire side of her property. It was a smaller mesh that had been there before, would be proof against any dog not prepared to try and jump it, which her Labradors would not.

It would contain her dogs, but it couldn't contain the growing sense of guilt that she felt, *knowing* she had been unconscionably rude, unacceptably thankless. The feeling ate at her until she gave in.

CHAPTER THREE

FIONA paused at the gate into Dare Fraser's property, just for an instant wondering if she really ought to do this. In the bed of her station-wagon, the borrowed fencing bar lay, inanimately accusing, the superficial excuse for her task.

She straightened her shoulders, wincing at the pain caused by the movement.

'I've got to do it, and the sooner the better,' she told herself.

She was considerably changed from two hours earlier, having spent a luxurious time bathing, washing her hair and scrubbing away the ground-in evidence of her weekend's labour.

Her fingernails were still a disaster; only time could repair the worst of the damage there. And her knees... well, the dirt might come out eventually, along with the variety of cuts, bruises and other minor injuries.

The physical damage, including the blisters which kept her fingers gingerly cramped around the steering-wheel, would heal with time; that didn't worry her. But her feeling of guilt could only get worse with time.

'And well you know it, too,' she muttered aloud, easing off the clutch to put the vehicle in motion again. In the deepening darkness, the road before her seemed vaguely threatening, overshadowed by the flanking rows of radiata pine and Lombardy poplar.

Again Fiona paused, the revealing moonlight giving her a choice of routes. She could discern a gigantic shearing shed, seemingly dozens of other outbuildings, and then, finally, the bulk of the enormous homestead itself.

Even in the uncertain light, it was impressive although, like her own new home, well-hidden from the highway. A two-storey structure apparently constructed of huge sandstone blocks, it loomed taller as she approached, dominating its surroundings.

She pulled to a halt in the circular driveway, self-consciously glancing down at her fresh, clean T-shirt and trousers, shaking back the loose mane of her hair.

Even after her bath, she felt grotty. Or else it's just guilt and nervousness, she thought. I am not looking forward to this, but I guess there's no way out of it.

Turning off the engine, she practically flung herself out and walked determinedly to stand before the tall, carved front door.

She made a fist, wincing at the pressure on her blisters, and knocked loudly before noticing the heavy brass knocker just above her head.

For a moment there was only the silence around her. Not even a dog had barked at her arrival and now she found herself wondering if Fraser was home. She was reaching for the knocker, determined to do it properly this time, when the door suddenly opened.

But it wasn't Dare Fraser!

The woman who stood looking down at Fiona was nearly his height, and, Fiona couldn't help but admit, was at the very least classically beautiful.

A model. And if she wasn't she should have been. Raven-black hair, loosely styled, spilled over her shoulders but was brushed back from a high forehead. Catlike eyes of a startling green peered from beneath perfect eyebrows, perfect lashes in a haughty, almost aristocratic stare.

The woman stood there, arms folded across a revealing *décolletage* with, Fiona couldn't help noticing,
perfect fingernails of extraordinary length.

Classic beauty! The hair, the dress, the make-up, the
stance—this woman had it all. Fiona kept her ruined
hands at her sides as the woman finally spoke.

'You wish?' And even from the two words she picked
up a hint of an accent, though not enough to guess at
the origins.

'Mr Fraser, if he's available,' Fiona replied, wishing
now that she'd left this chore until some other time, *any*
other time. The woman's entire attitude accused her of
interrupting something.

'It is ... important? He is ... busy right now.'

Too busy for you, the voice implied. And also,
somehow, implied just what he was busy at. And the
accent, Fiona decided, was probably Spanish, or perhaps
Latin American.

'I ... I just wanted to return something,' she began to
explain. 'I didn't mean to intrude.'

'It's no great intrusion,' came that husky, too soft
voice, and Fiona looked up to see Fraser's tall form
looming up behind that of his ... guest?

'I've brought back your crowbar,' she began lamely,
then strengthened her voice along with her resolve.
'Thank you very much for the lend of it.'

And despite the difficulty, the lack of privacy for such
a disclosure, she was about to add her apology for being
such a boor. Fraser gave her no chance.

'There was no need to return it this promptly,' he replied, 'although I'm sure you'll be glad to see the last
of the thing, from the look of your hands.'

Easing past the tall woman who slid gracefully, sen-
suously to one side, he stalked down the stone steps to
reach into Fiona's vehicle and heft out the heavy bar.

He leaned it casually against a porch support, then turned back to address Fiona.

'We were just having a drink, and you certainly look as if you could use one. Will you join us?'

The *last* thing she wanted, but before she could say so he was taking her arm and guiding her into the hallway. Behind them, his guest closed the door, then followed with a silent tread.

The room they entered was first off the hallway on the left, an enormous yet somehow intimate room, typical of its period and appropriately decorated in leather furniture and heavy, beautifully carved wood.

'I'll just introduce you two, then see about that drink,' Fraser said, turning to his tall, beautiful companion.

'Miss Consuelo Diaz...Miss Fiona Boyd.' The two women nodded, murmuring appropriate civilities, but each was aware beyond any doubt that there was nothing civil about their immediate reaction to one another.

The green cat's eyes of Consuelo Diaz flashed arrows of blatant contempt and condescension; Fiona simply felt overwhelmed by the other woman's elegance because she, herself, was so conscious of the ravages of her weekend.

'Fiona's my new...neighbour,' Dare explained as he turned to hand Fiona a well-filled brandy balloon. 'She's been busy all weekend building kennels.'

The explanation roused only a casual lifting of one perfect eyebrow, as did his continued dissertation, which to Fiona's astonishment ranged across her entire time in Hobart; her hobbies, her dog-training business and her television work—all got a mention in Fraser's potted biography.

Only the mention of the television work seemed to draw a glimmer of interest, and Fiona felt she'd have been totally dismissed by the elegant Diaz woman had it not been for that.

But worse was the fact she was given no opportunity at all to apologise for her rudeness, not that she expected to under the scrutiny of those glass-green eyes. Not now, she decided. Not in front of this woman!

It was, she decided, unnerving enough to listen to how much Dare Fraser had found out about her in such a short time, to wonder why he should have undertaken such a thorough investigation.

But to make her planned apology now? No, she decided. And worried even more because this was the first time in her adult life that another woman—any woman— had managed to make her feel, well, gauche!

Fiona knew she was attractive enough. She brushed up quite well, and did so regularly enough for her own taste just to handle the requirements of her work. But she had never been a clothes-horse, had learned to use make-up properly more through necessity than desire, and had never found fashion more than peripherally interesting.

But this Consuelo Diaz, she thought, must *live* for fashion, for physical perfection. The woman's skin, a creamy olive tone perfect for her ebony hair, was flawless even without the exactly applied make-up. Every stitch of her clothing was just right for her, had obviously been created *specifically* for her.

All of which made her a perfect match for Dare Fraser's immaculate grooming, for the tailored dinner-jacket, the dark trousers with their razor crease, the shoes with their military perfection of shine.

His rugged good looks and athletic bearing set off the woman's elegance, emphasised her beauty, made her classic sense of style all the more stylish.

All of which combines to make me look like the stablehand, Fiona thought to herself, contriving to hold the brandy balloon with appropriate dignity and hide her work-ravaged hands at the same time.

It was a waste; Consuelo Diaz had noticed them immediately and her clumsy attempt to disguise the damage now drew Dare Fraser's attention, as she ought to have known it would.

She was staring into the brandy, still shaken by the man's extraordinary study into her background, when the glass was suddenly plucked from her fingers and her right hand grasped gently but firmly by the wrist.

Fiona could only force herself to meet his eyes as Dare turned over first one hand, then the other, before staring down at her, head shaking as if he were admonishing a child.

'Are you a masochist, or just immune to pain?' he asked, surprise evident in the softness of his voice.

'Neither,' Fiona replied bitterly. 'Just short on time. I only had the weekend to get finished in; tomorrow it's back to work as usual.'

'More time than brains, I reckon,' he muttered in reply, thankfully keeping his voice so soft that only she could hear. But he spoke louder when he excused the two of them and steered Fiona out into the hall and along to where a bathroom held a thoroughly stocked medicine chest.

There, she was thrust impatiently into a chair as Dare carefully examined her fingers one by one.

'I suppose you're at least smart enough to have kept your tetanus shots up to date?' he asked roughly, though his fingers were incredibly gentle as he smeared first one, then another ointment into her fingers and the blisters which had now started to throb unmercifully.

Fiona nodded, but wasn't sure he even noticed. Nor did he notice when she tried to resist the light gauze dressings he wrapped round each hand at the base of the fingers, where the blisters were worst.

'You'll keep these on until morning, at the very least,' he ordered. 'Longer, if you can manage it, although I suppose if you're on camera tomorrow night they'll have to come off.'

'I'm not,' she muttered in reply, not that it was any of his business. The dressings would come off as soon as she was home, whether he liked it or not.

'Good.' He grunted his reply, but his voice softened to an entirely different tone as he continued. 'But if you *do* have to, make sure they keep the camera above here.'

And his fingers traced a slow, entrancing line from one shoulder to the other, touching like a tendril of ice across her collarbones, ice that turned to fire as his eyes burned into her own.

Fiona couldn't move. She sat there, mesmerised as much by his eyes as by his touch, as much surprised by the gesture as by the incredible physical effect it had on her.

Their eyes met, locked, held.

For one incredible instant she thought he was going to lower his hand, to take her breast into those strangely gentle fingers—as she suddenly wanted him to.

For another, she thought he was going to bend down and kiss her, and her lips were shaping for the kiss while her mind was steeling itself to resist it.

Or both.

Then the instant was lost, thrust away into oblivion with the lightest of scratches outside the door, with the sound of Consuelo Diaz's voice lilting, 'Daaaarling, we are going to be late, I'm afraid.'

Fiona jumped to her feet, thrusting away Dare's fingers as she scuttled towards the door, unwilling to look at him, afraid to speak.

His touch was on her like a brand, an unwelcome, unwanted brand. But, like his voice, memorable now, unforgettable even.

Fiona swung open the door, oblivious to the pain as she closed her fist around the handle. She forced her spine straight, forced herself to smile calmly at the face of the woman who stood, one dark eyebrow raised, looking down at her as she passed.

'Thank you for the medical attention,' she forced herself to say to Dare Fraser, who followed her from the room, followed her down the hall to the front door. 'I'll take more care next time.'

And she would! More care wherever he might be involved.

She held her poise until she was in the station-wagon, until she'd carefully started the vehicle, carefully driven round the circular driveway, carefully avoiding the gleaming sports sedan whose ownership she needn't question.

But by the time she reached the shadowy aisle of trees that formed his main driveway, Fiona was shaking. And she kept shaking, kept feebly brushing at the tears which insisted on forming at the corners of her eyes, until she finally reached her own driveway, finally halted the car and stumbled back to close the gate, shutting out the world, but not the unwanted memories of the evening.

She heard the throaty growl of the sports car as it passed in the darkness while she was walking back to the house, heard it but tried not to think of it as she thrust her key into the door.

'Damn,' she muttered. And repeated the curse as she lurched through the welcoming dog pack, for once not warmed by the enthusiasm of the dogs' riotous greetings.

The brandy no longer warmed her tummy; it burned inside her with a fire fuelled by bitterness, by embarrassment. Walking angrily to the bathroom, she stared glumly into the mirror, seeing the tiredness in her face, the weariness in her posture. Seeing also the thrust of her breasts, the hardness of her nipples with their individual memories of the wanting his touch had created.

But seeing also the elegance she could never match, would never—normally—want to match. Annoying!

She slept fitfully that night, her rest broken by spasms of conscience, moments of wakefulness. Her body, racked by the efforts of that weekend, was also affected by the spectres of her dreams, the memories of Dare Fraser's touch.

Morning brought little improvement. She woke late, had to hurry through her ablutions, didn't have time to give the dogs more than a perfunctory exercise run before rushing off to work.

And throughout the morning, she kept finding her mind wandering, kept finding herself thinking not so much of Dare Fraser himself, but about how he had managed to learn so much about her so quickly. And why.

'Perhaps he fancies you, although I can't imagine why,' said her lawyer, grinning at her across his desk without a hint of chagrin about being asked to give up his lunch-break just so Fiona could pick his brains on the subject.

'Somehow I doubt it,' she replied, refusing to be drawn to the bait. 'But there must be *some* reason for it, John.'

'I'm sure there is,' he replied. 'And most likely it's the logical one—you're a new neighbour and Fraser quite rightly was curious.'

'More than just curious—downright nosy is what I'd call it.'

He shrugged. 'Same thing. Don't forget you're living in the country, now. People in the country *like* to know about their neighbours. It's important.'

'Well, I don't like it.'

'Well, there isn't much you can do about it, is there?' was the reply. 'It's hardly against the law or anything, and besides, you haven't got heaps of skeletons in your cupboards... or have you?'

Fiona winced inwardly. Her earlier marriage and the messy divorce that had followed were matters of public record—in Queensland—but she had never mentioned either since coming to Tasmania, not even to John.

'Nothing but a raft of ex-husbands,' she replied lightly, 'and certainly nothing that's any of Dare Fraser's business.'

'And of course you're not at all interested in knowing Fraser's background, are you?' Her lawyer was looking at her with a suspicious glint in his eye, and this time Fiona couldn't resist the bait.

'Every gruesome detail,' she admitted, leaning forward eagerly in her chair.

His laugh was almost sinister. 'I thought you'd never ask.'

By the time Fiona got back to work that afternoon, she had an entirely new perspective on her neighbour, and most of what she'd learned did little to ease her suspicions that Dare Fraser might yet prove to be a serious problem in her life.

Her lawyer hadn't needed to breach any confidences in compiling a detailed dossier on Fraser; it had been more a case of just gathering in threads of common knowledge.

'Hobart's just a big country town, really,' he'd said. 'In fact, you could say much the same thing of Tasmania as a whole. Anybody who's anybody knows anybody else who's anybody—and your new neighbour certainly meets all the criteria.'

Indeed he did! Dare Fraser, she found, was a classic example of Tasmania's landed gentry. His family went back to the early days of the island's settlement, and his property had been passed through generations of Frasers.

'And your little block is the only bit that's ever been sold; the old families here didn't believe in such things,' her lawyer had said. 'There's a story behind it, but very few details. This Boyd woman apparently lived there with her brother, who was a worker on the property. He was killed in a tree-felling accident nearly forty years ago, and Fraser's father, for whatever reasons, partitioned off the block and turned it over to her. There's some suggestion that he felt responsible for the accident, but nobody seems to know for sure.'

There had also been rumours, he'd said, that Amanda Boyd had been the older Fraser's mistress, 'Although,' he'd cautioned, 'I wouldn't be mentioning such a thing if I were you. It's possible, of course, but...'

'None of my business and of course I wouldn't mention it,' Fiona had replied. 'But the real issue, I gather, is that Fraser wants the land back now just because it used to belong to his family?'

'That's my interpretation, anyway. These old families have fairly rigid ideas about things like that.'

'Well, you could hardly blame them. I'd imagine with so much tradition involved there *would* be very strong feelings about such things.'

But it was neither history nor tradition that caused Fiona the most concern. It was the present—and Dare Fraser's place in it.

Dare Fraser, it seemed, had spent most of his adult life in South America, returning when his parents had died within a week of each other a year earlier.

He had stepped into his inheritance with strong views about the responsibilities involved, and already was being spoken of as a force to be reckoned with.

His range of interests had been wide, according to John, and had covered various aspects of agriculture and land development. But he'd also been deeply involved in urban renewal and planning aimed at improving the lot of the rapidly increasing numbers of urban poor.

Fraser was described as a man of strong principles, a truly broad general education, and the character to be involved, rather than sit on the sidelines and reap the benefits of other people's work. A leader, a man who would forge his own path in life, but it wouldn't be a path that involved treading on those less fortunate, from what was said.

'The family's always been heavily involved with local government,' her lawyer had said. 'Both his father and grandfather were wardens of the municipality, and the word is that your man might be looking for a place at the next election.'

'He's not *my* man,' Fiona had retorted, but her heart hadn't been in the argument. It was hardly surprising that Dare Fraser was so knowledgeable about the council's regulations; she'd best be very, very careful to ensure her new kennel block couldn't be faulted. And she'd best get the kennel licence business sorted out *before* her neighbour's powers increased.

Not that it mattered much; if Dare Fraser wanted to make things difficult, he was already more than capable!

Such thoughts did nothing to make her afternoon go smoothly, although she did manage to organise a meeting with the council's planning officer for the next afternoon, and was thankful for the split-shift roster that allowed her the flexibility to do so.

The meeting, surprisingly, was much less stressful than she had expected.

'You'll have to advertise regarding the kennel licence, of course,' she was told. 'But considering your location and all, I can't see much to worry about.'

And the plans for the kennel block itself were approved without argument, which surprised and delighted Fiona. She had expected all sorts of bureaucratic nonsense, and was pleased to find the enforcement of the new regulations relatively straightforward.

She stopped in town on the way back to work and arranged the appropriate advertisements, secure in the knowledge that Dare Fraser would have to *work* to stop her plans in that direction.

Which, it appeared, he wasn't about to do anyway. She got home that night to find a note on her door which suggested her neighbour wasn't nearly the obstructionist she'd expected.

'Phone me tonight. Concreting on Friday... could do your kennel block at same time,' said the note, and when she *did* phone, it was to find Fraser as good as his word, although not long on explanation.

'Simple enough, I'd have thought,' he remarked to her plea that she couldn't afford his generosity and her query at just *why* he was being so helpful.

'It isn't simple at all,' she replied. Fiona was finding Fraser's involvement in her affairs terribly difficult to cope with. She didn't dare trust him, didn't want him being given so many opportunities to become involved, but she could find no logical way to avoid it.

'Of course it is,' he said. 'Watching you the other day reminded me that my own kennels could stand a touch-up, and if we share the costs of the concrete it makes things cheaper for both of us. What could be simpler than that?'

'But I've told you...I can't *afford* it right now, whether we share costs or not. I just can't afford it!'

'So square it with me later; the benefits are the same.' She could almost see him shrugging, could more than easily visualise him shaking his head at her obstinacy.

Recognising her opportunity, Fiona jumped at it.

'But I'm already indebted to you quite enough,' she said. 'You lent me the crowbar, you've actually *lied* for me, which I still don't understand, you helped me lay out my kennels, and now you want to help build them as well...'

'None of which is being more than neighbourly,' he replied, a trace of impatience coming into his voice. 'So if you can't handle that, just consider that I'm protecting my own interests. I want to be damned sure your dogs aren't going to hassle my sheep.'

Fiona gasped. Anger flared like a burning torch, just as, she quickly realised, he'd intended it to. But when she spoke, it was in carefully modulated tones, all sweetness and light and logic. Bastard!

'I really don't understand how lying to the police for me could possibly protect your interests,' she began. Lamely, at first, then more strongly as her conscience got its stride. 'But I certainly do want to thank you for that. In fact, it's really the reason I dropped round the other night, to thank you, and to ask you *why*?'

'Because that particular walloper is a decidedly officious and nasty piece of work,' he growled, voice sliding into the peculiar accent of rural Tasmania when he dropped the slang term 'walloper' into his reply.

Fiona couldn't help but grin. It was such *rural* slang, almost unheard nowadays on the Australian mainland, yet coming from the worldly Dare Fraser it sounded, somehow, just right. And the policeman *had* been officious, no doubt about it.

'He wasn't that way after you came along, thankfully,' she said. 'So thank you again; I was starting to feel quite uncomfortable at the time.'

'Forget it,' was the brusque reply. Fraser's voice was suddenly all business. 'I'll have my men round tomorrow or the next day to box in for the concrete; does it matter to you if you're there or not, and if it does can you give me a time that suits?'

Fiona was so startled by the transformation in his voice that she stumbled over her reply. What had happened? It was as if he had suddenly decided he didn't want to be overheard, or something.

'Yes...no...well...' she began, then more solidly added, 'No, I suppose it doesn't matter if I'm there or not, since you did the planning, after all. I'll make sure the dogs are locked in the house if I'm not, so you're not bothered.'

'Excellent,' was the blunt reply, followed by an even blunter goodbye. The telephone was hung up from his end before she could echo his dismissal.

Fraser's strange behaviour worried her through the little that remained of her evening, but didn't disturb her sleep, although for some reason it was right there to confront her in the morning and lasted through a work day that had little else to excite her interest.

Fiona found herself wondering about the various things she'd learned, despite having so little real information on which to make judgements.

Was there some reason, however remote, that the coincidence of names was somehow involved? Had the original Miss Boyd actually been *involved* with the elder Fraser, and if so had Dare Fraser known? And perhaps most important, why the splendid 'good neighbour' act, when it seemed perfectly obvious and logical that Dare Fraser should want her gone—not more solidly ensconced on land he wanted for himself!

Too many questions and not an answer to be found.

She arrived home after work on Thursday night to find the framing boxwork all done and her fencing panels carefully stacked to one side in preparation for the next day's work of getting the concrete laid.

But there was neither note nor telephone call from Fraser, nor did he answer her own phone call to him.

She got home on Friday night to find the concrete had been poured, had been properly levelled and screeded and her drains correctly shaped, and even the fencing panels and gates bolted into place.

Still without communication from Dare Fraser.

She spent the weekend fumbling her way through the 'pre-cut, pre-measured, a child could put it together in ten minutes' treated pine shed that would serve as her dogs' sleeping accommodation, but still heard nothing from Fraser and still couldn't contact him by telephone.

After the last fiasco, she didn't even consider driving over in person to thank him, and knew without actually admitting it that she would hang up without speaking if the dulcet voice of Consuelo Diaz were to answer his telephone.

For Fiona, her feelings towards the other woman were both surprising and a bit alarming. She had *never* in her life been intimidated by another woman, much less so instinctively wary and antagonistic. Even the dozens of young bimbos her first husband had been involved with so blatantly... but no, she wouldn't think of that. It wasn't at all the same thing, and...she just *did not* think of it!

'And I won't, either,' she muttered aloud, mentally damning herself for the stupidity of giving such thoughts life. 'Like "don't think of a white horse",' she snarled even more angrily, quoting what had to be the most ridiculous advice ever offered a curious child.

Because given any choice, any at all, she would *never* think of Richard! Handsome, charming, ruthless, deceitful, treacherous Richard, with his lies and his destructive ways, with his tarts and whores, his drugs and his drink. So plausible, *so* believable, *so* utterly evil he'd almost destroyed her.

But he hadn't. And, Fiona thought as she shook her mane of bush-honey hair, he wouldn't! Not ever! And neither, she vowed, would any other plausible, believable man. Nor any man at all, for that matter.

Sunday evening, having started on that note, could only get worse, and it did. Her mind in an overdrive of bad memories and worse, she struggled through the evening before trying vainly to sleep her way out of it all.

On Monday morning, having slept little and rested not at all, she locked the dogs away in their new quarters, drove in to work, and spent half the morning composing a brief, polite, non-committal note thanking Dare Fraser for his neighbourly assistance and asking what her share of the costs would be.

She put it in the mail during the lunch-break, lest she change her mind. It was chillingly polite, almost rude.

But very, very effective. Fiona got an equally polite note in the mail several days later, stating costs and charges but making no attempt, thank goodness, to renew any form of neighbourly contact.

It stretched her budget to the utmost, but she had a cheque in the return mail and was able to attend an obedience dog trial that weekend with just enough petrol to get her home and to work on Monday morning.

And the next couple of weeks weren't much better. She was forced to discover new and frightening aspects of budgets and financial planning just to keep food on the table and her vehicle on the road.

Still, she thought as she woke to brilliant spring sunshine and a work-free Saturday, it was all worth it, worth every penny. Lala was now fully in season, and the security of the new kennels was decidedly welcome. Fiona had originally planned to mate the yellow bitch this time round, but was now in two minds about the situation.

Certainly the budget didn't hold the two hundred dollars or so she'd need for a stud fee, but that had to be weighed against all the other circumstances, not least the fact she had firm orders for at least half a dozen pups.

On the other hand, the improving spring weather would mean an upsurge in interest in her dog-handling classes, and the last thing she wanted was a litter of pups and not enough time to properly socialise them and begin their formal training as working gundogs.

She rolled out of bed, scorning even breakfast on this most beautiful morning. Too nice to waste time brooding, too nice to do more than gulp down a cup of coffee and get outside with her dogs, she thought.

They quite obviously agreed, and the next hour was spent casually walking the boundaries of the property, Fiona occasionally hurling a retrieving dummy into a handy patch of scrub and the three dogs fiercely vying to see who could find it first and return it to her.

Then she got into the more serious aspects of their training, laying out patterns for directional work and trying to convince Trader that barking was not allowed when he was tied up to await his turn.

It was, she thought, about like trying to convince the sun not to shine, and Fiona was about ready to get heavy with the young dog when a change in the tone of his bark made her turn to see what was wrong.

The sight of Consuelo Diaz, resplendent in the most fashionable of riding gear, made Fiona immediately sorry she had chosen to work from Fraser's side of her property, with the dogs being tied to the boundary fence when not working.

'Too late now,' she muttered, and forced herself to wave to the approaching figure on the tall bay horse. Consuelo didn't return the gesture, but rode closer in silence until she was able to look down upon Fiona from an imposing height, the look holding obvious disdain for Fiona's less than fashionable jeans and sweatshirt.

The two women stared at each other for what seemed to Fiona to be hours, and clearly Consuelo Diaz was determined not to be first to speak.

Bother this, Fiona finally thought to herself, and greeted the other woman with a civil 'Good morning.' The gesture brought her only a curt nod; Miss Diaz's attention was diverted to Trader's anxious attempts to crawl through the fence and visit with the horse.

'You'd only get yourself kicked halfway home. Now settle down and stop being such a twit,' Fiona muttered at the writhing chocolate figure, which, as usual, ignored her.

The horse, too, seemed intrigued by the dog's antics, and stepped closer to the fence, long head bowed to snuffle at the excited animal.

Consuelo Diaz yanked sharply at the reins, digging spurred heels into the horse's flanks as it twirled away. Fiona, immediately angered by such treatment, had to swallow the criticism that leapt to her lips. It wasn't her horse, she determined, nor her business how the older woman handled it.

The rider's slit-eyed silence, moreover, was decidedly unnerving, despite the fence between them and the fact Fiona was on her own land, minding her own business, and perfectly entitled to do so.

And when Consuelo Diaz did finally speak, the message in that lilting, unusual South American accent was only too clear, if not entirely logical.

'You should not be here; this is no place for you here,' the woman said without preamble.

And then, instead of replying to Fiona's startled 'Why?' she spurred the horse round and cantered off without a backward glance.

'How very strange,' Fiona muttered to the dogs, who all stood to attention, eyes fixed on the departing figure. They, of course, didn't answer either, but at least their attitudes were friendly.

'That woman really doesn't like me,' Fiona said to herself as they all strolled back towards the house. What she couldn't figure out, since the only logical reason—jealousy—was clearly *illogical*, was why!

By the time lunch was over, the incident had lost its impetus. It could hardly be important, Fiona had decided she could exist quite happily without Dare Fraser or his exotic girlfriend and her dislikes.

And the less I have to do with either one of them, the better, she thought. I can be a perfectly good neighbour without getting involved any further.

It seemed a splendid theory when she went to bed, but when she was awakened at dawn by a growling, slavering monster that was trying to smash down her back door, there was at least a brief moment when a handy neighbour might have had great appeal.

Amid the pandemonium of her dogs going mad, she dashed to the window, gasped in astonishment, then flung open the door and rushed outside, adding her own voice to the fray.

Unfortunately, Lala followed right on Fiona's heels, and since Lala was the focus of all the commotion her presence did nothing to help.

'Get out! Go on...get out of it!' Fiona cried, brandishing the broomstick like some modern-day witch as she charged down off the back porch in pursuit of her intruder.

Devilish eyes peered at her as the ghastly beast scuttled away, but the brute's attention was divided between Fiona and the yellow bitch whose aroma was so entrancing to the stray dog.

Fiona rushed. The stray easily slipped away to one side, those bold eyes laughing at her. Again she rushed, and again the animal flowed away from her, this time turning swiftly as it tried to entice Lala to join it.

Hampered by her nightgown and bare feet, Fiona pursued the fiend in what seemed to be ever-diminishing circles, but eventually realised she wasn't going to catch it, wasn't going to drive it off while Lala was clearly in evidence, and was in real danger of having her careful mating plans go up in smoke.

'Lala—*heel*!' she finally cried, abandoning the visitor for the moment as she tried to divert her dog's attention from the shaggy, fleet-footed suitor.

To her great relief, Lala obeyed, and was quickly shut inside the house. 'Now, little mate, we'll sort *you* out,' Fiona cried, once again lifting the broom as she stalked forward.

What followed would have been funny had it not been so serious. Fiona, still in her nightgown and bare feet, chased the stray back and forth and round and round, while Trader and Molly charged around their kennel like dervishes, barking and growling their encouragement.

She thought for an instant about turning Trader loose, then as quickly discarded the idea. He was too young, had never fought another dog, and was unlikely to be a match for this shaggy mongrel that was half again his size.

'If I had a gun, you wouldn't be smirking, you mongrel bastard of a thing,' she gasped at the strange dog, which now seemed to be laughing as it easily dodged her assaults.

'I think I prefer you with your broomstick; it's much more in character,' interrupted a voice from behind her, and Fiona shrieked with alarm, spun around, and slipped on a damp patch of grass, to land in a welter of flying bare legs and broomstick squarely at Dare Fraser's feet.

'And, just for the record, he's neither a mongrel nor a bastard,' Fraser said, grinning hugely as he reached down to lift Fiona to her feet, eyes roving insolently over her near nakedness as he did so.

'He's both, and so are you!' Fiona hissed as she tried to wrench free.

'He's in love; you should show a bit of compassion.'

'Compassion? I'd sooner give him a lead injection,' she replied, struggling in his grasp. 'Will you let me *go*, dammit?'

'Why? So you can hit me with your broomstick? I've got to protect my dog, after all. He's the best sheepdog in southern Tasmania.'

Fraser's grip had shifted, somehow, from Fiona's arms to her waist. What had been a gesture to help her to her feet now became a holding action, not quite a caress, but close enough that she felt the difference, and knew he did also.

His fingers were like fire against her waist, burning through the scanty fabric of the nightgown. As he looked down into her eyes, Fiona was suddenly over-aware that she hadn't combed her hair, or brushed her teeth, that she wore no make-up at all, that her nightgown was worse than useless as any sop to modesty.

Fraser's fingers moved, ever so slightly, but the movement became of itself a caress, and the laughter in his eyes changed to something far more threatening than laughter.

Fiona's body was responding to his nearness, to the touch of his fingers, the expression of...lust?...in his eyes. No, she decided immediately; it wasn't lust, but something quite different, something infinitely more complex.

Looking past his shoulder, she could see the snout of his utility vehicle in her driveway, realised he'd driven up without her even noticing. And realised she was now hopelessly within his control, like it or not.

'Will you *please* let me go?' she pleaded, unwilling to meet his eyes, afraid of her body's reaction to his touch.

'It'll cost you a cup of coffee,' he said, and the laughter in his voice rippled through its depths. 'It isn't often I have to chase old Blue through this kind of dawn caper, and,' his voice altered subtly, 'never with such a...an unusual ending.'

And before she could think to reply he'd released her and was striding off to his vehicle, whistling the shaggy sheepdog in behind him.

'You might put some clothes on, too,' he growled over his shoulder. 'Damned difficult to make an appropriate apology if I'm too distracted.'

'Apology...my foot,' Fiona muttered as she rushed for the house and the questionable sanctuary of her bedroom. Whatever the situation, the great and glorious

Dare Fraser was enjoying every minute of her discomfort, and didn't even have the decency to deny it.

As she threw on her clothing and quickly ran a brush through her hair, she heard him enter the house, speaking softly to Lala as he did so. And without even so much as a growl from the treacherous, deceitful bitch, Fiona thought fiercely.

It was worse when she finally entered the kitchen to find he'd put the kettle on, was spooning out teaspoons of instant coffee, and Lala was fawning round his feet as he did so.

'Some watchdog you are,' Fiona muttered aloud. 'You're supposed to have his leg off, not fall in love.'

'Don't be so unprofessional; she can't help her hormones any more than my poor old sheepdog out there,' Dare grinned. 'There's no reason she has to be a man-hater just because you are.'

'I . . . I'm no such thing,' Fiona replied, caught on the hop by his smiling assessment.

'Which . . . unprofessional or a man-hater?' And the grin was even wider now. He had her going and he knew it.

Fiona fumed, but held her tongue until she had exactly the reply she wanted.

'Neither, as a general rule. Although there would likely be exceptions to the first and I could *make* exceptions to the second,' she said sternly.

Dare Fraser seemingly ignored the jibe. He silently poured boiling water into the two cups, added milk and sugar without asking, and passed one cup over to Fiona.

'Here. Get your blood sugar boosted a bit; it might improve your disposition,' he said with yet another grin.

'There's nothing wrong with my disposition,' she replied sulkily. 'Or at least nothing that *not* being exposed to mongrel bloody stud dogs at the crack of dawn wouldn't cure.'

Dare Fraser shook his head sadly. 'And you supposed to be the dog expert,' he said. 'Blue isn't a mongrel; he's a *Smithfield.*'

And before she could say, 'There's no such proper breed,' she was being given a history lesson about Tasmanian sheepdogs.

CHAPTER FOUR

With their third cup of coffee, Fiona walked out with Dare Fraser for a closer look at his mongrel that wasn't, her animosity mostly forgotten in her fascination with the tale she'd been listening to.

It had been fascinating, but did little to alter her first opinion about the dog's inherent ugliness. He was, at first glance, something like an Old English sheepdog—if an amazingly scruffy one—but with a tail. And with colouring that was somehow not quite right. Fiona thought for a moment, then realised he was actually more like a bearded collie than an Old English, but certainly not a show specimen as she understood the term.

'He'll never win any beauty contests,' she said with a shake of her head as the shaggy creature peered at her.

'Your little bitch mightn't agree,' was the provocative reply. 'Just shows there's no accounting for taste, I suppose. Besides, he's a working dog, not a show dog.'

'I'd always thought they were a *type* of sheepdog, rather than a specific breed,' she countered. 'Certainly they're not a registered breed for show purposes, not recognised by the national kennel authorities.'

'You're a chauvinist, did you know that?' Dare's accusation interrupted her thought, and the very word he'd used at first confused her.

'What on earth are you talking about?'

'Chauvinism, in the true sense of the word. You're so hung up on the purity of breeding lines and the like that you're blinded by the original purposes involved.'

'I am not! I'll admit to being concerned about breeding integrity, but I certainly am neither hung up about it, as you crudely put it, nor blind.'

'Humph! I just hope you're a little more open-minded when it comes *your* turn, or I pity the poor beggar you choose to sire your children.'

Fiona was unconscionably affected by this teasing turn. Her first instinct was to bridle at the man's effrontery, but she also found herself wanting to shy completely away from such an intimate subject.

Her mouth, as usual, let her down.

'I'm hardly likely to choose a husband the way I would a stud dog,' she retorted, even as she realised this was no way to change the subject.

If Dare was offended by her brusque reply, he didn't show it. 'There's a lot to be said for it, actually,' he replied with a slow grin. 'You'd probably want a fairly well-set-up sort of fellow, to be sure your boy children had the chance to be that way, and you wouldn't want anybody too awfully ugly, or your girls might suffer.'

Fiona was silent; she didn't like the way this was shaping up, not one bit. Dare, on the other hand, was quite clearly enjoying his flight of fancy.

'I mean, after all, there's no sense being as pretty as you are and then marrying some homely boy-next-door type and producing girls you have to provide dowries for to get them off your hands.'

'Oh . . . stop being ridiculous,' she complained. 'There are far more important things than physical beauty, even when you're breeding dogs. And with people, well . . .'

'All things have to be considered,' he countered. 'Even physical beauty, although I agree it's hardly at the top of the list.'

'Well, I'm *so pleased* you agree,' she replied. 'Not that I expect it matters very much, since I'm not planning marriage, much less a family, in the foreseeable future.'

'Ah, but then you never know, do you?' Dare grinned. 'For all you know, your knight in shining armour might come riding up any day at all, without any warning. And you'd have to be ready, or you might just miss out.'

'I won't hold my breath.'

'Of course not; you'd turn blue, which might be your colour clothing-wise, but I somehow don't think it would be quite right for your face,' he jested, and raised one dark eyebrow when he failed to get even a smile in reply.

Fiona didn't know what to say. Already the subject was bringing up memories best forgotten, memories she did her best *to* forget. And Dare's levity did nothing to ease the pain of those memories, much less to help her feel at ease discussing the subject.

'Can we just change the subject?' she finally asked, hoping directness might give her a way out.

'We could, but why, I wonder? Is marriage and having children such an unpleasant topic for you? And if so, I wonder why. Is it because you've got a boyfriend tucked away somewhere... or maybe even a husband?'

He knows, she thought, and shivered inside. Not that it was any great secret, but for some reason she would rather have been able to tell Dare about her previous marriage, not have him find out from other sources.

'Or is it that you don't like discussing it with a poss- ible candidate, I wonder,' he continued, his grin now broader, more knowing.

He *doesn't* know, she thought, and inwardly breathed a sigh of relief. Then wondered why she should be so relieved! He wasn't a candidate; she didn't want or *need* a candidate as either a husband or the father of her children.

'And if I did, it certainly wouldn't be you,' she muttered, then gasped as she realised she'd spoken aloud. Dare Fraser merely laughed at the *faux pas*.

'Wouldn't it, now? And why not, I wonder? Am I too old, too young, not tall enough, too tall, or is it just that you don't fancy the colour of my eyes? Not very complimentary so early in the morning, are you?'

Fiona saw the laughter in his eyes, but try as she might she couldn't see the same humour in the situation as he did. Her ears heard his jibes, but it was her entire *self* that related to his mocking questions. And she was quite suddenly faced with the fact that her self could find little if any fault with Dare Fraser, at least from a physical point of view.

He was, in his own terminology, well set up, and was— if not classically handsome—certainly good-looking. Fiona didn't even need to look at him; she knew the colour of his eyes, the strength of his jawline, the set of his broad shoulders. And she knew there was no really safe answer to his bantering teasing.

'This early in the morning, you're hardly an improvement on your mongrel of a dog,' she finally countered. 'Maybe you can argue on an empty stomach, but I can't. And more coffee would only make it worse, so I suppose I'll have to offer you breakfast and hope that'll get rid of both of you.'

Dare's grin was almost boyish and certainly infectious. 'I thought you'd never ask,' he retorted, and led the way to the kitchen as if he hadn't eaten in weeks.

Thankfully, he dropped the subject of marriage as he sat at the kitchen table watching Fiona prepare bacon and eggs and toast and marmalade in quantities that would have kept her for several days on her own. But his silent appraisal was almost as bad; it was as if he was making a calculated study of her abilities in the kitchen.

But when she finally put the meal on the table and sat down across from Fraser, he opened the conversation not with food but with dogs.

'Tell me a bit about this training you do,' he began. 'Is it just confined to conventional obedience, or gundog work, or what?'

Fiona laughed, comfortable now the conversation was on familiar ground. 'It's *people* training, if you really want to know,' she said openly. 'I hardly train the dogs at all; I train their owners, and hopefully, occasionally, *they* train their dogs. In theory, that's how it works.'

She wasn't prepared for Dare's chuckle, much less for the question that followed.

'And do you use your broomstick, or a cat-o'-nine-tails, or just your sunny disposition?'

Fiona paused, fork half raised to her mouth, which she knew was open. Then she lowered the implement and stared hard at her guest, before allowing herself a slow smile and a shake of her head. Damn the man! He seemed able to get her goat without even half trying and, worse, he was enjoying it.

'I use motivational training methods, for the dogs,' she finally replied, wallowing in her ability to remain calm for once. 'For the people, it's more a matter of being a combination drill sergeant and outright tyrant, most of the time.'

And when he didn't immediately reply, but merely nodded in apparent understanding, she resumed eating while keeping a careful eye on him. A most disconcerting man!

'You ought to try feeding them,' he finally said, lifting his fork in a small salute. 'This is really very good, not least when you consider the way you were invaded this morning.'

'Hardly an invasion,' Fiona replied, acknowledging the compliment with a slight bow of her head.

'Well, a distinct inconvenience, at the very least,' Dare said. 'And one that I propose to make up to you, if you aren't too busy this evening.'

'This evening? I . . . I *did* have plans to . . .' Her lame attempt at excuse-making was quickly forestalled.

'To wash your hair, I suppose. That's usually the quickest excuse, but in this case it won't wear,' Dare replied sternly. 'You've fed me and I shall return the favour. Your hair, or whatever it was, can wait. There's a brand-new Chinese restaurant in the city that's begging to be tried, and I have no intention of going alone.'

'I wasn't trying to make excuses,' Fiona lied. 'It's just that, well, I *do* have an early start tomorrow and I was a bit concerned you had something planned that would involve being late, that's all.'

His look said he didn't quite believe her, but he merely nodded his acceptance with a slow, almost gentle smile.

'Good, that's settled, then. And I promise to make sure my dog's locked up, too, although I'd suggest you keep little missy here in the house just to be sure. There are occasional strays, and even a two-metre-high kennel wouldn't stop some of them. Not in the circumstances.'

'That's why she's been sleeping with me,' Fiona replied, and couldn't help adding, 'Although she's *supposed* to be a watchdog, as well.'

'Obviously she knows I'm no threat,' was the reply, but it was delivered with a mischievous grin that gave Fiona no room for complacency.

'I think it's more that she gets to be something of a tart when she's in season,' she replied. 'Anything male and she's fair game.'

'Not like you,' he muttered. Or she thought he did.

There was no chance to ask; already he was on his feet and marching to the sink, his mind obviously on other things.

'I'll wash,' he said. 'It's easier that way, because you know where everything has to go once it's dried.'

'Don't be silly,' she began to object, but to no avail. He'd already flung open the cupboard beneath the sink and found the dish soap, and had begun stacking things into the sink.

'Not silly. I'm a top washer-upper,' he said. 'Not a bad cook, either, though hardly in your class, I expect. I'm spot-on with any kind of meat or fish, but I still have trouble with veggies; probably 'cause I don't eat as many as I should.'

'That's dumb,' she replied without thinking. 'Any damned fool can throw vegetables into hot water until they're cooked, surely.'

'That's a very chauvinistic answer,' he retorted, hands now buried in the sudsy water. 'How, for instance, do you know when sweetcorn's cooked just right and ready to eat?'

Fiona absently reached for the plate he was finishing, struck dumb by the simplicity of the question. She had cooked sweetcorn often enough, but the exact answer eluded her.

'Well? Do you time it, or what?' Dare handed her another plate and assaulted the rest with vigour as he waited for her answer.

'By the smell!' she suddenly cried. 'You know it's done when it *smells* done.'

'Brilliant. And what does it smell like when it's done? Like burnt tyres, or seared mutton, or——'

'Well, it smells like...like...well, like sweetcorn,' she stammered. What a silly question, not that the answer was much better.

Dare seemed unimpressed. *Was* unimpressed.

'And you, of course, know exactly what sweetcorn—cooked—is supposed to smell like?' he retorted. 'Typical feminine reaction, but hardly of much use to somebody faced with the problem for the first time.'

'That's not fair! And anyway, it's a silly example. There are far more common vegetables than sweetcorn, and they're easier to cook, as well.'

'Maybe for you; I prefer to let other people resolve those particular mysteries, as I shall tonight,' he replied, now seemingly bored by the discussion. 'Speaking of which, what kind of Chinese food do you like best?'

It was an easy way out, and led to a sprightly discussion of the merits of Singapore fried noodles versus conventional noodles, whether various duck offerings should be boned or simply chopped up Chinese-style, and whether honey prawns should be sweet or savoury.

More important, it continued until the dishes were done and Fiona could logically expect the departure of her visitor.

'I'll collect you about six, if that's OK,' Dare said as he was leaving. 'Thanks very much for the brekkie; let's hope dinner can be as splendid.'

'I'm sure it will be,' Fiona replied, thinking to herself that her comment was likely a lie, regardless of how good the food might turn out to be.

And as she worked her way through the necessary weekend chores, it was difficult to concentrate on such mundane things as washing clothes—*and* her hair—in view of the prospects ahead.

'It's not as if it was a date, not really,' she muttered to the dogs as they followed her from laundry to clothesline and back again. 'He's just paying me back for breakfast, that's all.'

She didn't really *want* to think of it as a date. Dare Fraser was far too volatile for her to want him involved in her life—especially not romantically. She didn't need romance, she told herself. Didn't need it and didn't want it, especially not if romance would—as it must—involve the heady physical reactions she'd already found in Dare's presence.

It would have been easier, she decided, if he'd remained the enemy she'd expected, instead of the good neighbour he seemed determined to appear.

In the same breath, she chided herself for being too trusting and not trusting enough, unable to come straight out with the admission that the man had given her no reason at all *not* to trust him.

'Yet!' she said, meanwhile sorting through her wardrobe for something appropriate to the occasion and cursing herself for not asking him about that when she'd had the chance.

Trousers were definitely out, although it had always been her impression that most Hobart restaurants were fairly informal at the best of times. She didn't want to be too dressed up if he arrived in very casual gear, but on the other hand...

'Always better a little overdressed than under, Mum always said,' she told herself, and finally chose a fairly simple dress in not-quite-basic black that could be dressed up in an instant with a fairly flamboyant Liberty scarf if required. It was neither startlingly low-cut nor terribly modern in fashion, but she had always liked the way the soft jersey fabric looked on her.

And for her hair? Fiona debated only an instant. Fraser had never seen her with it other than in a ponytail, and she saw no good reason to change that. So it was for no good reason that she twisted it back into a simple chignon that added elegance to the length of her neck.

'Ridiculous,' she muttered into the mirror. 'It isn't even a date—not that it should be, either.' So, to make up for that one gesture, she dismissed out of hand the lightly patterned black tights that had caught her eye only the week before. Better, she thought, the faintly smoky-coloured ones; patterned tights required near-perfect legs.

It wasn't a sentiment shared by Dare Fraser, who arrived exactly on time, looking casually dashing in an open-necked shirt beneath a splendidly fashioned Harris tweed sports jacket, dark brown trousers and dress boots that were polished to a mirror-finish.

That he approved of Fiona's costume was obvious; his eyes roved across her features and figure with an expression that approached possessiveness, and he nodded his head in patent approval.

'I think perhaps I've chosen wrongly,' he said in a soft, appreciative voice. 'You look far too nice for where we're going; perhaps we ought to switch to the Casino or the Sheraton, where you can be properly appreciated.'

'You promised me Chinese, and that's the deal,' she replied, inordinately pleased by the compliment, but also just a shade uncomfortable at the thoroughness of his scrutiny.

'Were you a dancer, once?' he asked, totally changing the subject and confusing her further in the process. And at her denial, completed the process by commenting, 'It must be all the walking round after the dogs, then. You don't get truly splendid legs like that without exercise. I'm glad you've the sense to avoid those bloody awful new-fashioned patterned tights, too. They're only fit for girls with legs that wouldn't be noticed in the first place.'

Fiona didn't dare risk a reply. She could feel herself blushing and wished it were possible to stop on command.

Once inside the gleaming BMW that lorded it over her ancient station-wagon in the driveway, she tucked her legs hard in against the warm leather of the seat, half wishing she'd worn trousers, secretly delighted she hadn't.

Dare drove, as she would have expected, with a seemingly casual expertise, but in a rather surprising silence that Fiona made no real effort to break. It wasn't until they were in the city and parked in front of the restaurant—just as if he'd reserved the space beforehand, she thought—that he turned towards her and startled her with an apology.

'I think I embarrassed you, and I have to apologise for that,' he said. 'Take it that I was overwhelmed by the change from when I first saw you this morning.'

'That isn't an apology, but I'll take it as one,' she replied, cocking one eyebrow and forcing herself to meet his not-quite-mocking grin. 'If I'd known you were that taken with before-and-after concepts, I would have really got dressed up.'

'You are,' he replied, and slid out to come round and hand her out of the car, giving her a feeling of such real and unexpected pleasure she almost curtsied. Nor did he let go of her hand, but held it with light but firm familiarity as he escorted her into the restaurant.

The place was far from typical, the designer having for some reason avoided the usual red-flocked wallpaper and Chinese lanterns so usual in oriental restaurants.

Subdued lighting, equally subdued décor and splendidly professional service combined to let Fiona anticipate a truly memorable evening.

The headwaiter's suave comments of greeting added to the impression, but hardly in the fashion she had expected. Almost immediately, the oriental gentleman's words spelled out with certainty that Dare Fraser was a liar!

The fact hit Fiona like a hammer-blow, and she still hadn't recovered several minutes later, when they'd been seated and Dare was explaining himself with far too glib an apology.

'It was only a little white lie,' he said. 'I don't even know for sure why I bothered, except to try and maintain a sense of spontaneity that seemed fairly important at the time.'

Fiona didn't reply. Her sudden coolness had prompted the apology; she had turned to ice when the headwaiter had directed them to 'Your usual table, Mr Fraser.'

It wasn't the lie she minded, but she couldn't tell him that, couldn't explain that it was the gesture, the sheer glibness of the exercise. It was so...so *Richard*. The shadow of her ex-husband fell over the evening like a shroud, and nothing Fiona could do or think had any influence.

Dare, to his credit, also tried his best, but the damage was done. For the second time—that she knew of!— he'd lied, and the professional smoothness of both occasions had now raised a spectre she couldn't bury again.

The first course had come and gone before he chose to become serious about the subject, which only made matters worse.

'You really have a thing about personal honesty, don't you?' he asked with startling directness. 'Which means you've more than likely been a victim of lies, and not just white ones, I'd suspect.'

He didn't, she realised immediately, really expect a detailed answer. Which was just as well, because she was *not*—definitely not—prepared to give him one. Nor was she prepared to lie about it, so she did the next best thing and simply nodded her agreement.

'And you're not going to talk about it, so I can presume there was a man involved, and no, you don't have to answer or even nod,' he continued, holding her with his eyes. 'I'm just speculating out loud, for what it's worth. I do a lot of that, sometimes.'

The arrival of the honey prawns, brown and succulent and smelling heavenly, was a welcome interruption from Fiona's viewpoint. She devoted herself to the tricky business of handling them with chopsticks, and used the time gained to pray that Dare would change the subject.

He didn't. But he did the next best thing, which was to revert to silence as he, too, attacked the prawns with just the dexterity she would have expected. His large, muscular hands coped with the chopsticks as if he'd used them all his life.

'Did they have a lot of Chinese restaurants in South America?' Fiona asked, speaking the words just as they came into her mind and then halting, wide-eyed, as she realised what she'd done. Never once between them had the subject of South America ever been raised. A fool would realise she'd been checking up on Dare's background, and her host was no fool.

But instead of the anger she expected, he put down his chopsticks and grinned hugely, delighted either with her *faux pas* or just at having caught her out.

'You're just full of surprises, aren't you?' he chuckled, clearly enjoying himself. 'It's a pity we didn't realise earlier there was all this mutual curiosity—we could have got together and sorted it out without having to resort to old-boy networks and gossips.'

Fiona didn't answer. What, after all, could she say?

'Stop being so solemn,' Dare said sternly, grinning at her and waving his chopsticks in a parody of orchestra conducting. 'There's nothing wrong with curiosity, provided you're not a cat. Which you, my girl, most certainly are not.'

He paused to capture another honey prawn and masticate it thoroughly, almost sensually, before speaking again.

'OK... you can have first go,' he said. 'Anything you want to know and I promise not to so much as *bend* the truth, not even a whisker. My life's an open book anyway, but you couldn't be expected to believe that, I suppose.'

'What's the *real* reason you wanted my property so badly?' Fiona could have bitten her tongue, but it was out now, having lingered on the fringes of her mind virtually since the auction sale, if not before.

And she wasn't prepared, not at all, for the reaction.

Dare's eyes hardened perceptively, became darker, became almost frightening. She could see the muscles along his jaw tensing, could feel the tenseness all the way across the table.

He put down his chopsticks, with no smile this time, and Fiona braced herself for an explosion she felt sure must now ensue. But then, even as she watched, the intensity faded, and when he spoke it was in perfect calm, perfect control.

'The place used to be part of my farm, but I expect you know that,' he began. And to her absolute astonishment, he then launched into a tale that held her transfixed, the food almost forgotten except when he paused deliberately and forced her attention on the sumptuous morsels which kept appearing on the table.

'And of course you know that you're not the first Boyd to live there, although you're marginally the prettiest.

Amanda Boyd, you might be interested to know, would have given you a close race in her younger days, in the days when I knew her, when I was a child.

'She's the reason, or part of it, why I left Tasmania at the age of seventeen and didn't come back until just over a year ago. My father was the rest of the reason.'

'I...I...don't think I want to hear this,' she began, but was sternly overruled.

'You asked for it, and you're *going* to hear it,' he said, and his voice was bleakly cold, icily severe. 'You're the only one who's ever heard it, and—unlike you—I'm trusting enough to believe it won't go any further.'

'I...no, please...' Fiona *didn't* want to hear it, didn't want to hear even another word, and yet...

And Dare Fraser, damn him for his sensitivity, for his uncanny ability to almost read her mind, caught that minute hint of weakness. And pounced.

'Curiosity, thy name is woman,' he misquoted ruefully, shaking his head ever so slightly as his mobile mouth curled down with a wry twist.

'Amanda and her brother Ben lived in that house right from the time I was a baby,' he continued then, eyes half closed in recollection. 'Ben worked for us, and they were practically family. Then Ben was killed in a tree-felling accident. I was just little and I don't know the details, except of course that it left Amanda, who would have been eighteen or nineteen, with no family and no place to go, really.

'I don't know to this day if my father was responsible for the accident, or if he just felt that way, but for whatever reason he partitioned off your house and the ten acres and they became Amanda's. Which would be fair enough, if that were all that was involved, but it wasn't.'

He looked at Fiona then, a direct, open stare that left her almost prepared to believe he was opening himself totally, putting total trust in her.

'By the time I was twelve or thirteen, and old enough to sort of understand these things, it became fairly obvious there was more to it than just guilt.'

'Surely you're not saying...' Fiona couldn't finish the question. The mental image of a teenage boy growing up with his father's mistress living just across the paddock, almost within shouting distance, left her cold. And the effect on the boy's mother... Fiona visibly shuddered.

'Did your mother know, or suspect?'

'She knew! Or at least I think she did. It was never put in so many words. But when I was thirteen I was forbidden ever to set foot in *your* house again, or to speak to Amanda, who was virtually a maiden aunt to me.' Dare gave a brief flick of his head, the expression in his eyes evidence of the pain this must be causing him.

'And my father backed her up, so there must have been something to it all.'

'But... but surely this Boyd woman wouldn't have stayed, not knowing...' Fiona stammered through the half-completed question, fumbling with the confusion it all raised.

'She was a proud woman.' Dare's eyes softened in some unspoken memory, his voice softening with them. 'And so very, very beautiful. She was a schoolteacher, and a good one, I suspect.

'I don't know if there was any suspicion outside my own family; certainly I never heard so much as a whisper while I was growing up.' He once again shook his head, mouth twisted in bitterness. 'But then I wouldn't have, would I?'

Fiona saw in his expression the confused, tortured youth he must have been, and her heart went out to him, almost to the point of reaching across the table to take his hand. Then she caught herself, and halted the gesture in mid-reach.

'I rather think you would have,' she said, head cocked in speculation. 'In fact, I'm sure you would have. You'd have been living in a very small, tightly knit society back then, I'm sure, and it just doesn't seem logical that there could have been very much going on without half the countryside knowing about it.'

Dare shrugged. 'In retrospect, I feel much the same, sometimes, and—again with the benefit of hindsight—I often wish I'd disobeyed my parents and gone to Amanda to find out for myself.'

Fiona's smile was tinged with uncertainty. 'Frankly, I can't imagine you *not* doing so,' she admitted. 'But I suppose you had your reasons.'

She didn't add that such reticence was completely at odds with the perceptions she had of Dare Fraser the man, but his quick glance revealed that she didn't really have to.

'Hah! But then you don't know that I didn't hit my really rebellious stage until I went away to school,' he said.

'I wasn't thinking of that, so much, but about the recent past. You had plenty of opportunity, surely, between the time you returned to Tasmania and the time she died,' Fiona mused.

'I only saw her the once in all that time,' he admitted somewhat ruefully. 'She didn't attend my mother's funeral—logically enough, I suppose—and she didn't attend my father's, for reasons I can't guess at. I did try and visit her, but to be honest she wasn't the Amanda Boyd I knew as a boy, and, well, I guess I'm not subtle enough or something. I tried to bring up the subject gently, but it didn't work at all. She kept confusing me with my father and bringing up conversations about things I knew nothing about. She was suffering from Parkinson's disease, and I really don't think her mind was any too clear most of the time.'

Fiona shivered inside at the thought of a poor, sick, old woman alone in that isolated house, perhaps looking to death as a release. But as a release from what? From conscience? Or just from the vagaries of old age, sickness, perhaps even senility?

'Did...did she die there? At...well, at my house, I mean?' It was a question that for some reason had occurred to Fiona for the very first time only that instant, and she was just as surprised by it as Dare Fraser appeared to be.

'No...she was in hospital,' he replied. 'I...I'd been sort of keeping an eye on her, as much as I could from the distance she wanted to maintain, so I know that much.'

He shoved away the final bits of his meal and leaned back to light a cigarette and then stare at Fiona, his dark eyes hooded with thoughts she couldn't begin to read.

'Would it have bothered you greatly if she had died at home?' he finally asked. 'I can sort of see why it would; my parents both died at home, but that's quite a different thing, I should imagine.'

'Bother me? No, not really,' she replied after a pause to think over the question. 'Not as much as the loneliness she must have suffered, at least some of the time. It's strange, though, that of all the vibes I get from the house there's very little of loneliness.'

'I'm not surprised; she was very strong, a very self-reliant woman,' Dare replied softly. 'Much different towards the end from how I remember her from my childhood, obviously, but admirable for all that. She was just so used to doing for herself, she couldn't come to terms with seeking help or even accepting it.'

'I can understand that,' Fiona said without thinking, only to find herself forced to think by his blunt reply.

'I'm sure you can, being much the same type of person.'

It wasn't so much the comment itself, she decided, but the almost bitter confidence with which he made it.

'I certainly don't see anything wrong with being able to take care of oneself,' Fiona replied, perhaps a bit too strongly. 'It isn't *that* unusual in a woman, surely?'

'Not unusual, except when it's carried to extremes.'

'Which you're suggesting I do? Rather an *unusual* attitude from a man who's been responsible for half my fencing and most of my kennels,' she retorted. 'What *is* your argument? Haven't I thanked you properly... or what?'

'Neither of the above,' Dare replied quickly. 'I have no argument—none whatsoever. All I did was make a comment, damn it! There's no reason to take my head off for it.'

'I'm not taking your head off,' Fiona snapped. 'It's just that I cannot *stand* being on the receiving end of an anti-feminist dissertation just because I won't lie down and be a doormat for anybody.'

'Nor should you. Not that I could ever imagine you doing so, but I don't think I'd like you nearly so much if you did,' he replied with a hint of a smile. Then the smile widened as he added, 'The doormat part, anyway. I can't be certain I'd object to your lying down, at least not in the right circumstances.'

Fiona blushed. It was something she almost never did, but this time the reaction caught her before she could even begin to think of the appropriate snappy reply that could save her.

Dare's grin widened, grew more devilish as he savoured his victory.

'That wasn't exactly fair, was it?' he said then. 'I'd recant, except that I meant it, so you'll just have to put it down to excess chauvinism and when you get home you can make up a voodoo doll and stick pins in it or something.'

Fiona's mind was whirling, working overtime to find a way to get away from this conversation without giving Dare yet another victory. She started to speak, halted, then began again.

'That's far too complicated for such a minor offence,' she finally said. 'I'll settle for boosting the bill tonight with some total sweet extravagance...like fried ice-cream, unless you're determined to settle me into a witch's mould, of course.'

His laugh was totally relaxed, his eyes also smiling an acceptance. 'Better I share your extravagance, I think,' he said, and turned away immediately to signal up the waiter.

The order given, Dare excused himself, and when he returned it was to change the subject entirely to something—from Fiona's viewpoint—that was eminently safer.

And, equally important, he kept the conversation on safe ground throughout the rest of the meal and even on the drive home, talking about farming, sheep, his time in South America—anything and everything but personal relationships.

And as they drove home he gradually lapsed into a sort of preoccupied silence that quite suited Fiona's own mood. The unexpected delving into Dare Fraser's very personal experiences was starting to prey on her mind;

she wasn't at all sure she liked having done so, yet somehow felt privileged at the same time.

It was, she thought, dangerous knowledge to have!

But when they arrived in her driveway to a brief but vocal reception from the two dogs in the kennel and a muted echo from inside the house, Dare showed no remorse at having confided in her.

'Thanks very much for listening tonight,' he said instead. 'I feel better about all that, having got it off my chest.'

'I'm glad,' Fiona replied, then halted, uncertain what else, if anything, she might say.

'You should be,' he replied with a grin. 'It wasn't until we really got into it that I realised how much I'd let the thing fester inside.' He paused, then added, 'You're a good listener, which helps.'

This time Fiona merely nodded in acceptance of the compliment. Dare suddenly seemed too intimate, too close, in the confines of the car.

'Thanks for having dinner with me,' he said then. 'And next time I'll try not to disturb your morning lie-in as badly as Blue did this morning.'

'It doesn't matter,' Fiona said as she got out of the car. 'And thank you for dinner; it was lovely.'

'No better than breakfast,' he said waving. 'See you on the next trip.'

Later, snuggled into her bed with Lala snoring on the floor beside her, Fiona felt at peace with the world. It wasn't until the next day, with the arrival of the postman, that everything started to fall apart in a screaming heap!

CHAPTER FIVE

FIONA took one look at the company letterhead on the single envelope that comprised her morning mail and knew even before she opened it that it just couldn't contain good news.

How right she was...how horribly, frighteningly right. The letter inside marked the end of her future as she'd planned it, destroying all her hopes and aspirations in a welter of carefully worded clichés that did little if anything to soften the blow.

Her lease was expiring and it wouldn't be renewed. Her school, unless she could find a new venue, was going to end just as she was getting truly, properly, established.

She read the letter again, and yet again. But each reading gave her only the same horrible verdict.

She couldn't believe it...*wouldn't* believe it. Her entire future had just gone down the drain.

'What can I do?' she asked John the solicitor for the first time and herself for the thousand-and-first as she'd stumbled through the first part of her day in a daze of shock and worry.

'On the face of it, not very much at all,' her lawyer replied after his usual careful assessment of the facts involved. 'They need the warehouse for other purposes and your lease is about to expire. Unless you know a particularly effective prayer, I'd say your dog school is about to make a move.'

'But where to? I'm in the middle of a semester now, and if I'm forced to comply with this letter I'll have no place to hold the final class,' she raged.

'I don't wish to be accused of saying "I told you so",
but when you signed this lease I remember telling you
this problem might occur,' he said enigmatically.

'But they were quite clear that my evenings were no
problem at all,' Fiona cried.

'Then! Things have obviously changed, and you're in
no position—legally—to argue. Morally, you might have
some case, but financially the arguing of it would be
hardly worth your while,' he said.

'But what am I going to do, then?'

'Why not run it from home, at least temporarily?'

Fiona started to argue, then stopped herself. He was
right, of course, now that she gave it a moment's
consideration.

'Do you think I could?' She asked the question rhe-
torically; already her mind was awhirl with ideas of how
she could run her dog school on her own property, under
her own conditions, her own demands.

'I don't know. Most of that would be up to you. Living
on ten acres, with no close neighbours, you might be
able to push it through council,' John said. 'But there
would be complications, I'd expect—things like development applications and the like.'

'But I *could* do it?' She found herself astonished at
how quickly the concept thrust itself into consideration.
To be able to run the school from home! To be able to
finish the last class of a winter evening and just *walk*
home! It was an invigorating thought.

'Provided you don't have any problems with your
neighbours,' John said with a grin. 'And that shouldn't
be too difficult. Nobody objected to your kennel licence,
and I gather you're on fairly good terms with the most
important of your neighbours, at least.'

Fiona didn't blush. She might have, on the basis of
the previous evening's experience, but having now taken

the time to read the latest edition of the *Sunday Tasmanian* she was far less inclined to expect any help from Dare Fraser.

'You obviously didn't see the weekend *Tasmanian*,' she said with a bitter twist to her voice. 'The last thing my *best* neighbour would do is help me organise a dog-training school next to his precious bloody sheep!'

'I did read it, and I think you're over-reacting just a trifle,' her lawyer replied calmly. 'There wasn't a single thing in the article to suggest he'd automatically be opposed.'

'He would!' Fiona knew she sounded almost child-ishly petulant, but she just couldn't help it. Reading the article in question on top of her crisis situation had robbed her of any optimism. The interview with Dare Fraser had touched both on his South American experiences and on his attitudes toward urban/rural land development at home, and the clarity of his position could do *nothing* to produce optimism in her case.

One of the major problems in areas of South America, he'd said, was that major landholders controlled too much land, leaving potential peasant farmers with no hope of securing a future in their own country.

In Australia, by comparison, the encroachment of "hobby" farmers into viable agricultural land was causing a severe problem, according to Dare. Pressure from many local councils was forcing landholders near suburban areas to cut up their lands for urban or semi-rural development, and the loss to the agricultural economy was significant.

'The councils want an expanded rating base, which is fair enough,' he'd said. 'But every expansion of urban development into agricultural areas brings a host of problems, not least of them the loss of land for agri-cultural use.'

He'd gone on to list some of his pet peeves, most of them issues Fiona herself agreed with. Roving packs of urban-based dogs, insufficient bushfire precautions, poor land management with regard to noxious weeds...all significant!

She could just imagine his reaction to a proposal involving stacks of untrained dogs being landed right next to his sheep, especially since she now realised the paddock directly next door was the one he favoured for his lambing.

'You ought to know better than to let your heart rule your head,' John was saying, but Fiona barely heard. The other thing which had drawn her attention in the weekend paper was a fashion photo-article which featured the classic beauty of Consuelo Diaz; she could hardly have missed it, since it was directly opposite the interview with Dare Fraser!

'I...what on earth are you talking about?' she cried as John's words finally sank in.

'Well, quite obviously something!' he replied. 'What's come up between you and Fraser that you can't even go and talk to the man about this?'

'Nothing,' she replied hotly. Which was true as far as it went. She wasn't about to get involved now in a discussion about how averse she was to being any further in her neighbour's debt.

'Good. Because it would do no end of good to have him on your side in this, as I'm sure you realise. So...are you going to approach him, or do you want me to do it?'

'Oh, no!' She found herself mouthing the objection with hardly a conscious thought. If anyone would approach Dare Fraser about this, it would be Fiona herself, and there was much to be considered first.

'What am I going to do for money?' she asked then. 'I can't operate out in the open, especially not in the winter.' And especially, she thought, not with her neighbour's precious sheep grazing right within sight. 'I'll need some kind of a building, and the size I'd need doesn't come cheap, you know.'

A lengthy discussion involving the lawyer's calculator produced the consensus that Fiona would require a training shed at least the size of a four-car garage, perhaps five metres by ten. 'And that's cutting it fairly fine,' she said. 'Nine by twelve would be better.'

'It's a commercial situation; getting money—within reason, of course—shouldn't be that much of a problem,' John mused.

'Paying it back would very definitely be a problem,' was Fiona's response. 'I'm stretched pretty fine already with the mortgage, let alone adding another one.'

Which was a thought that she carried home with her, its having already dominated her mind throughout the day. She *might* manage, if she could add a couple of extra classes—and keep them! But it would mean a year of brutish work, combining the job with the career, probably fitting in weekend classes as well.

The problems and potential problems weighed heavily throughout the drive home, and finding Fraser's Blue panting expectantly at the back door did nothing to improve her saddened disposition.

'You want seeing to, me old mate,' she growled at the fawning Lothario. And, after a sweeping glance across the horizons suggested her neighbour didn't realise his prized sheepdog was on the romance trail yet again, Fiona decided the only way she'd get any peace would be to take the animal home herself.

'Come on—in you go,' she commanded, waving towards the open tailgate of her station-wagon with what she hoped was a suitable authority.

The dog crouched, obviously listening with but half an ear; the rest of his attention was focused on Fiona's back door and the amorous delights to be found there.

'In, damn it!' And to her surprise, the dog obeyed, if not with any marvellous show of willingness. Fiona didn't care whether he liked it or not; she slammed the tailgate closed before he could change his mind.

'Back in a flash,' she cried to her own dogs, who yelped their disapproval at the whole proceedings, and within minutes she was driving into Dare's yard, eyes flickering back and forth as she looked for his kennels.

It was the work of a moment to get a leash on the lovesick sheepdog and put him securely into a vacant kennel. Fiona was just turning to return to her vehicle when a sullen voice queried her presence.

The fashion plate that was Consuelo Diaz didn't wait for a reply. Instead, she launched into a verbal assault that left Fiona stumped for any chance to reply.

The machine-gun speed of the abusive commentary, combined with the woman's accent and the intricate switching from English to Spanish and back again, made it impossible for Fiona to decipher exactly what she was supposed to have done, but there was enough clarity for her to realise her actions would be reported to Dare Fraser, and *pronto*!

'Fair enough,' she muttered in reply, unwilling to put herself into an argument with this woman. Especially, she thought, since she would more than likely end up in the wrong, no matter what the facts.

'Tell him what you like,' she finally said, and was in her station-wagon and driving away before the reply could be sorted out. She didn't know whether she had been accused of stealing the damned dog or trespassing to return him, and after the day she'd had Fiona didn't much care.

All she wanted was a quiet evening, what was left of it, and early to bed without any further problems. What she got, astonishingly, was the privilege of arriving home to find that Blue was there before her!

'I do not *believe* this!' she cried, leaping from the vehicle with seven sorts of mayhem in mind. And even as she did so, the obvious explanation became distastefully clear.

'You witch of a woman,' she snarled in the direction of where she'd left Consuelo Diaz. 'I'm surprised you'd have the nerve to get anywhere near a kennel dressed like that.'

The model's fashion-plate outfit hadn't gone unnoticed; now its very chic seemed to sneer at Fiona.

And what to do now? She couldn't very well return the dog for a second time, not and have to face the risk that Fraser's woman would only turn him loose as soon as Fiona left. But the obvious alternative, that of waiting until he noticed the dog's absence and followed the logical reasoning, would certainly put paid to her chances of an early night.

'Damn it...damn it...damn it!' she cried. 'Why today, of all days? Why me?' And almost expected a sepulchral voice to give her an answer.

Looking round, realising it was almost dark now, she also realised she was running out of time for any decision at all. Her own dogs had to be fed, Lala had to be let out to relieve herself, and both activities required some adequate disposition of the amorous sheepdog.

'Right. It's back into the wagon with you, I guess,' Fiona said, flinging open the tailgate and fixing the dog with her most commanding glare.

'In ... now!'

'And let us pray he's been taught not to eat up-
holstery,' she muttered as she let out her dogs and
watched them rush to surround the station-wagon with
a chorus of abuse for the visitor.

From then on, it was easier. She fed her crew, locked
them in the house, and carefully put Dare's dog into the
kennels, where he could stay the night—if need be—in
safety. It was far from an ideal solution, but the best
she could think of at the moment.

Much later, when Fiona had changed into casual
clothes, fed Blue and eaten her own evening meal, a yodel
of greeting from outside was chorused by her own mob,
and she shouted 'Come in,' at the expected knock on
the door.

'You shouldn't to be this casual about visitors in the
middle of the night,' said Dare Fraser as he stepped into
the room and smiled gently at her. 'What if it hadn't
been me?'

'What indeed?' Fiona was in no mood to be sociable
with this or any other man just now. And her mood
wasn't improved by the fuss her dogs made over Dare.
'You can take your lovesick hound home any time,' she
said bluntly. 'And he's had his tucker, by the way.'

'Well, I'm glad *he* has,' was the reply as he walked,
uninvited, to sit down at the table across from her.
'What's the matter—had a rough day?'

'One totally unimproved by coming home to find
Romeo panting at the back door,' she replied, surly and
not caring who knew it. 'And I'm sure you'll be appropriately looked after once you've taken him home; just
see—if you wouldn't mind—that your ... your friend
leaves him kennelled, this time.'

'You've lost me,' he replied, raising one eyebrow to
accompany the query.

'I'm only saying that I've taken him home once tonight, and put him away in a kennel, and the bastard beat me back here! That's what I'm saying; it should be clear enough!' Fiona knew her voice was rising in anger, didn't care.

'Ah.' He was—damn him anyway!—just *so* calm and just *so* rational about it all. 'And you're suggesting, I gather, that Consuelo——'

'I never mentioned any names. For all I know you could have fifteen *friends* about the place who could have done it. The one you mentioned is the only one who spoke to me, and of course I didn't understand it because my Spanish, or whatever it is, isn't that good,' Fiona interrupted, running her own words together so quickly she could only just follow them herself.

'Well, I wasn't there, so of course I can't say,' he replied, eyes darkening. 'But I'm sure it wasn't anything deliberate——'

'Well, if it wasn't deliberate, then you'd better change that hound's name to Houdini,' Fiona raged, all pretence of her own temperament now flown. 'Now will you please, please, please just get out of here and take him with you?'

'I rather think I'd better,' Dare replied, rising easily to stand looming over her, dominating the atmosphere of the kitchen.

Fiona didn't bother to watch as he strode towards the door, but the sound of his voice forced her to look up as he opened it.

'I have to say this, trite as it sounds,' he began. 'I really *do* apologise for this. It——'

'I don't need apologies,' Fiona snapped. 'I need your bloody mongrel dog kept home where he belongs!'

The outburst washed round him like river water around a rock. Dare stood there, solid, unyielding, one dark eyebrow raised as he stared at the intensity of her outburst.

'Oh...look. I'm sorry,' Fiona sighed. 'It isn't you and it isn't the poor damned dog's fault, either. It's just that his randiness is one more problem I didn't really need today, that's all. Please, just take him and at least *try* to keep him under control.'

'I gather that I'm a problem you can do without today, too,' Dare remarked without rancour. 'But when you've settled down a bit, you might want to talk about it.'

And he was gone, quietly shutting the door behind him, before she could even think to reply. Fiona, for her part, stayed unmoving for long, long moments, partly ashamed of her outburst, but mostly just too weary to bother moving.

Fiona had the consolation that Dare kept his dog under control for the remainder of the danger period, but he didn't take her objections to include himself.

'I appear to owe you another dinner,' he said on the telephone a few evenings later. Not unexpected, but Fiona was none the less thankful that his timing allowed her to refuse because she had classes and then her late shift as excuses.

And even without such excuses she was far too busy. Every spare moment was taken up in drafting her development proposal to the council, planning the type of building she'd require to run the training school, and studying the various bylaws and regulations that might affect her.

It was a staggering expedition into the wilderness of the bureaucracy, and she was soon exhausted and heartily sick of it all.

'It's damned madness. Every time you turn on the news, the government's bleating about help for small business,' she raged at John during one of the increasingly volatile telephone calls that seemed vital every second day. 'But just *try* to do anything and all they do is throttle you with red tape!'

'Of course. Without the red tape, they couldn't justify their own existence, let alone yours,' he replied with typical cynicism. 'Most of it's only there for appearances' sake anyway; it shouldn't cause much problem.'

'It takes *time*,' she raged. 'Time I don't have. I'll end up losing a full semester over this nonsense, for sure.'

'Have you tried to get an extension where you are?' her lawyer asked. 'I'd have thought it worth a try, at the very least.'

'Of course it is. Only of course I'm too stupid even to think of it,' she cried. 'Oh, John, you're a darling, you really are. Now I have to fly. Lunch is nearly over and I'll have to try and catch the owner while I can.'

She nearly hung up on him in her haste, then furthered the delay by misdialling twice in a row the number she wanted. But when she finally did reach the owner of the warehouse where she'd been holding her classes, it was only to find she'd most likely been wasting her time all along.

'I'd probably be able to arrange it, except we don't own the place any longer,' was the explanation. 'I sold it, which is why I had to let your lease go. Settlement of the deal is the day after your penultimate class, and I'm afraid there isn't much I can do to help you.'

He could, however, provide, the name of the new owner, a company headquartered in the new Cambridge industrial park, but a company unknown to Fiona. It was also, unfortunately, unknown to Directory Assistance, which made further enquiries that day a wasted effort.

Nor did she do much better through the rest of the week; the new owner, it seemed, was a holding company for yet another holding company *ad infinitum*. In desperation, she was once again on the telephone to her friend and lawyer, who said he'd help, but not to be in a hurry.

'There's no sense being in a hurry any more,' she replied. 'I'm already reconciled to the fact that I'll probably die an old maid before all this bureaucratic nonsense with the council is finished.'

'And how are you getting on with that Fraser chap?' he asked, pointedly ignoring her anti-bureaucracy stance. It was a gesture which impressed Fiona as little as did his question.

'I do wish you'd stop pushing me at Dare Fraser,' she snapped. 'When I get my proposal together, I'll make sure he has a copy, and I'll make sure I discuss the whole thing with him, but not until then, if you don't mind.'

'Not up to me to mind,' was the laconic reply. 'It's just that he could probably be useful if you could get him on side; he isn't without influence in the district, after all.'

'I know that.' Which she did, of course. Fiona hated to be deceitful, even just by omission, but she couldn't come out and tell John the reasons behind her wish not to be further beholden to Dare Fraser. It wouldn't make sense to him, in the first place, she told herself. It didn't really make all that much sense to her, except in principle, which for the moment was quite sufficient.

Dare Fraser had too damned *much* influence, both in the community and in her own life, whether he realised it or not. And Fiona was quite sure he did realise it, and that knowledge didn't make her comfortable with the fact.

But as the days passed and the red tape grew thicker and more complex in its windings, she often felt it might be nice to have Dare Fraser's influence.

'The council wouldn't be stuffing him around with all these stupid regulations,' she muttered to herself. 'Or if it did, he'd know just how to short-cut things.'

Then she chuckled, amused by the mental picture of her neighbour wielding a mighty sword, slashing through the Gordian knot of red tape, sending bureaucrats flying in all directions.

The planners had promised they could get her development application through the council in three weeks or less; what they hadn't told her was that the complexity of it all would make the preparation take longer than that.

'I can't imagine what they do for projects complicated enough to have indoor plumbing,' she growled to John at one exasperating point in the situation. 'How do people get anything done in the face of all this nonsense?'

'With great difficulty, usually,' was the cynical reply. 'You have to remember that bureaucrats and governments aren't run for the benefit of the public; the public is really just a nuisance factor. Bureaucrats are run for the bureaucrats, not for you or me.'

'How could I forget?' Fiona replied with a growing cynicism of her own.

'I couldn't imagine,' he said. 'By the way, I've managed to track down the buyer of your warehouse.'

'Wonderful,' Fiona cried, 'or at least it would be if it weren't too late anyway. I've only the one more class and I've arranged to have the last one, the one I would have lost, at home the following Saturday if the weather's good.'

'Good,' he replied. 'Then this won't be of any interest, I trust.'

'Oh, but it will. I'm curious, now, about why all the secrecy. Of course, it wouldn't have anything to do with me, but still...'

'All right. I'll keep all this stuff until the next time you're in the office,' was the reply, and Fiona was sure she caught an unexpected note of caution.

'Please do. I may drop in tomorrow, if that's OK.'

'I was afraid you'd say that,' John sighed. 'See you then.'

And to her astonishment he hung up before she could even say goodbye, quite obviously wanting to avoid any further discussion over the telephone.

'How very strange,' she said to herself, and spent the rest of the day with curiosity niggling at the back of her mind. That same curiosity helped her through what should have been a disastrous evening of classes in which every human had two left feet and every dog a schizophrenic mode that switched haphazardly from terror to violence.

And at lunch next day, her own mood did likewise when she saw the information John had collected, when she realised who was behind the loss of her training building—and why!

CHAPTER SIX

'PLOT! It's got to be; couldn't be anything else,' Fiona raged, oblivious to the strange glances her behaviour was drawing from the table staff at the restaurant.

'I think you're being just a bit paranoid,' her lawyer friend muttered, his own voice low as if in compensation for her loudness.

'Paranoid? I'll give that damned Fraser paranoid!' Fiona was oblivious to her friend's natural reserve, to virtually everything but her own sense of betrayal and anger.

How could Dare Fraser be involved in such a thing? But, on the other hand, why not? He owed her nothing, not even any explanation of his involvement in the buying of the warehouse where she could no longer operate her business.

'There isn't the slightest bit of evidence he even knew you were involved in the place,' John continued, voice still calm. 'He's only listed here as a minority shareholder, after all.'

'Oh, sure,' Fiona sneered. 'And look who's the *majority* shareholder—that bitch of a woman from Chile, or Argentina or wherever. The one who hated me on first sight, who's done nothing but go out of her way to cause me problems. And you suggest he didn't know?'

'I'm saying there's no evidence at all to say he did know, that's all. Apart from the obvious documentary evidence that he's somehow involved in the business, all I've been able to find out is that he's the architect on record for the renovations. It could easily be that he's no more involved than that.'

'He's a hell of a lot more involved than that with Miss Consuelo Diaz, I can tell you that,' Fiona replied bitterly, and wondered just why she felt so utterly betrayed by all of this.

She poked idly at the rare-cooked steak in front of her, mixing pink juices with the butter that flowed from the baked potato. Eating was almost beyond her now; her stomach felt as if somebody had stabbed a knife into it.

John obviously had no such inhibitions; he chewed happily at his own portion of grilled flounder before bothering to reply.

'I really don't understand what makes you so outright suspicious of Fraser,' he finally said. 'The man's done nothing but help you, according to everything you've said. He didn't object to your kennel licence, even went so far as to help you build the damned kennels; he's dropped whatever scheme he might have had for buying the place out from under you, and still you go on about him.'

He paused for another bite, then spoke with mischief crinkling his eyes. 'If I didn't know better, I'd think you had some emotional thing going here.'

'I have not! And I wish you'd stop going on about it,' Fiona snarled. 'You're always doing that, and I'm sick of it, do you hear? I'm not interested in Dare Fraser or any other man, and, just for the record, I'm not jealous of Miss fancy-accent Diaz, either.'

'Hamlet, Act Three,' was John's cryptic reply, and Fiona looked up to see that he was struggling to contain the laughter that already had brought tears to his eyes.

'*This* lady doth *not* protest too much,' she snapped. '*This* lady just wants to get on with the business of running her life without interference. There's no emotionalism involved at all, unless it's plain, ordinary anger at being treated like a dumb blonde by Dare Fraser and you and...and...well, everybody!'

All of which, she told herself as she drove back to work, was perfectly true. Which didn't explain all of her feelings, but enough. She *wasn't* jealous of the dark-haired beauty of Consuelo Diaz, and she wasn't jealous either of the woman's relationship with Dare Fraser.

'I just don't like her; it's as simple as that,' she muttered at the dashboard radio. 'And she—quite obviously—doesn't like me either. Well, so what? Nothing on earth says everybody's got to like everybody else; some people just instinctively dislike each other on sight.'

And as for Dare Fraser? Well, John could obscure it in all the legal gobbledegook he wanted to, but *she* knew that Dare Fraser wasn't to be trusted, and that was that!

Which was why she could only stand there, open-mouthed and staring, when he stalked into that final evening's first class at the warehouse and stopped short to stand staring back at her.

Around her, handlers and their dogs faltered to a chaotic halt, the handlers spellbound by the vibrations of hostility, the dogs merely confused.

'What the hell...?'

'What are *you* doing here?' If Fraser seemed taken aback by the situation, Fiona was anything but. His appearance, however unexpected, served only to be a focus for her anger.

He didn't immediately reply, but stood there, tall and straight and somehow commanding, immaculate in freshly ironed moleskin trousers and a work shirt with the sleeves rolled to the elbows. He was also, she noticed, freshly shaven; the heathery scent of his aftershave seemed to form a scent-link between them.

In the corner, Lala wriggled in welcome, her tail thumping and a subsonic whine pleading for Dare's attention. Damn the bitch, anyway, Fiona couldn't help thinking. How can I keep him in his place with all my dogs in love with him?

'I'm really sorry,' he finally said. 'I just came to check on a few things; I didn't realise you were here training until I walked through the door.'

'I'll just bet you didn't,' Fiona replied, her eyes hot with scarce-subdued hostility.

'If I had known, I wouldn't have interrupted,' he replied, voice soft, condescending. And still he stood there, muscular hands on hips, somehow looming above the few other men in the vast room. 'I saw the lights, and...'

'You...you...' Fiona couldn't find the words. She was blinded, almost deafened by the explosion of her anger, a fury that was fed by her own reaction just to the sight of this man. Even as she hated him, she was drawn to his quiet calm, to the sight of the dark hair curling at the opening of his shirt, to the muscular set of his body.

How could he *have* such an effect on her? How could she *allow* him to have such an effect? She was suddenly conscious of her own clothing, of the too tight jeans, the too large sweatshirt, the old and battered sneakers, one with the fresh and odorous memento of an over-excited puppy.

And she was all too conscious, also, that Dare Fraser was seeing her, was seeing her clothing and somehow seeing beyond it, that his eyes took in the curve of breast and hip, the long line of her neck.

'Perhaps we ought to discuss this later, or at least outside,' he was saying in that too calm, controlled voice, and Fiona suddenly realised, or remembered, that they weren't alone, that others were hanging on every word,

every gesture. Not least of them the two attractive secretaries in their designer leotards, skin-tight and colour
co-ordinated, no less, to their designer Afghan hounds.
The dogs were their normal selves; the handlers fairly
drooled.

'We'll discuss it now,' Fiona hissed through clenched
teeth, and turned to bark 'Take a break!' at her startled
class. She strode towards the doorway, presuming Dare
Fraser would follow, *knowing* his eyes would.

Outside, she stopped abruptly, angrily flung off the
strong hands that shot out to steady her as she spun
around off balance.

'It's obvious you know something about this that I
don't,' Fraser said. 'So do you want to go first, or shall
I?'

'You go first,' Fiona replied without hesitation. 'Go
first and go damned quick. My lease doesn't end until
after tonight and I don't have to put up with your interference with my classes. And I won't! You can turf
me out after tonight, but you've got no right to interfere
now and I won't have it!'

'Nor should you, I suppose,' he replied, 'although I've
already apologised for interrupting. But what's all the
rest of this you're rabbiting on about?'

'As if you didn't know. Look, I'm busy; I've got no
time for you. Please just get out and let me get on with
my class, if you don't mind.'

'When do you finish?'

'When I'm done,' she replied, half truthfully and half
evasively. 'What does it matter?'

'Not a lot, if you insist on staying in this mood,' was
the reply. 'But I do think some explanations are in order.'

'It's a bit late for that, don't you think?' Fiona replied, her voice cold and her body rigid with what she
hoped came across as disdain. It must, she thought. She

just couldn't face having him *know* how strongly his nearness was affecting her, how easily it managed to sneak past her anger and her feelings of betrayal.

'Never too late,' was the laconic reply. 'And, since I'm here now, I think I'll just wait until you're finished. I'm not real fond of being rousted on in public for an honest mistake.'

'Well, you can damned well wait out here,' Fiona retorted, turning away as quickly as she could.

'I don't think so,' was the reply, and she knew he was following her.

'I said out here,' she spat, turning to claw at him in a futile, almost childish attempt to make her point.

'What are you going to do about it—make an even worse scene?' And he grinned, but there was no humour in the showing of those even teeth, just a grim determination.

'Oh . . . please yourself,' she grunted, turning away defeated and knowing she couldn't possibly win that particular argument. Dare Fraser was all too capable of making a scene, would probably enjoy doing so, she thought.

But, once inside, he quietly joined the small group of onlookers which Fiona normally termed her 'peanut gallery', thus transforming it, she thought instantly, into something entirely different and less easily described.

If only, she thought immediately, she could be halfway through the last class of the evening, instead of the first of three. Dare's presence threw her entirely off stride, and that was nothing to what it did for the nubile secretaries and their long-coated, unmanageable hounds. Fiona was in distinct danger of losing control of the class entirely, with the two women ignoring all else but Dare Fraser and their dogs sensing the switch of interest.

They're all bees round a honey-pot, she found herself thinking, mentally logging a firm declaration for future classes concerning appropriate dog-training attire. For a moment, she thought it a catty gesture, but then she stamped her foot—mentally. This was a dog-training class, not an aerobics class!

Just as well, too. Fiona's own equilibrium was shot to blazes by the man's very presence in the room. While the secretaries became sleeker and more agile for the mutual sharing of attention, Fiona found herself stumbling like a drunkard as she tried in vain to focus on the people, the dogs and the exercises.

The overall result bordered upon chaos, although Fiona knew that she alone realised it. Most of the class didn't know their left foot from their right, even into this seventh class, much less how smoothly things should be going—and weren't!

And the dolly-birds? They knew only one thing, and it was sitting watching, which was all they cared about.

As Fiona gradually restored a semblance of order to the class, she found herself growing increasingly furious with Fraser. How dared he come in and disrupt her class like this? She totally ignored the logical, reasonable part of her mind, the part that said, What's he doing? He's just sitting there, just like four other people. He isn't even paying that much attention to the secretaries and their Afghans, because he's mostly watching you!

And if he weren't watching me, I wouldn't be being so damned clumsy, I wouldn't be giving such contradictory commands, and I wouldn't be having all these totally distracting thoughts, she told herself. And admitted in spite of herself that she couldn't really blame the secretary-types for their attitude.

Hate them, maybe even find a way to punish them for it during the final class, she thought spitefully, but hardly blame them.

She was, in actual fact, more inclined to thank them for their frivolous hanging around after class. Their motives were shockingly transparent, but at least they kept Fiona from being alone with Dare until the next class began to arrive, this time with older, more experienced dogs, but also with one older, more experienced connoisseur of devilishly attractive, available men.

And this woman, too, seemed to go all weak at the knees just at the sight of Fiona's unwelcome visitor. It was more amusing than annoying, until the end.

Then, Fiona was hard put to it to avoid being shoved into a role of having to introduce the two. The woman's toy poodle didn't think that much of Dare, or any other person, for that matter, but his mistress was clearly smitten.

Maybe I *should* introduce them, she found herself thinking. If the poodle would let her, the old witch would fasten on him like a leech and drag him off out of here.

A fine fantasy, but there was no reality in it; if Dare had bothered to notice the woman, who did her best during the hour to ensure that he did, Fiona saw no sign of it.

Indeed, when the moment did arrive when an introduction might be seen as fitting, Dare had slipped out to his vehicle for a cigarette, and Fiona couldn't help but feel the move had been deliberate.

But he was back as soon as the woman and her poodle had gone, and it was immediately clear that something had drastically changed his mood.

'This isn't working at all,' he said without preamble. 'You need me hanging about here like a fourth hole in the head, so I'm going. But I definitely *do* want to talk this thing out, so if you'll pardon the cliché—your place or mine?'

'Mine,' Fiona replied quickly, almost shaking with relief at his decision. 'About nine-thirty or just a bit later, if that's OK?'

'Done,' he said. 'Have you had tea yet?'

She started to argue, but was immediately thwarted.

'I thought so. OK, it'll be pizza and beer, so try not to be too late or you'll miss out.' And he was gone before she could say another word.

Fiona stood, mouth open in surprise at his abrupt change of mood, but had to regain her composure quickly when the first student in her final class arrived almost immediately.

That final class, by comparison to the earlier ones, went amazingly well. Without Dare's hovering presence, Fiona was in full control of both herself and the class, and she finished bang on time without any problems at all.

Her mood didn't quite last the drive home, but neither did she arrive with the same surge of anger his arrival at the warehouse had precipitated. Indeed, when she arrived to find him roistering comfortably with her other two dogs, there was a brief and distinctly disturbing sense of pleasure in the sight.

She banished that as quickly as she could, reverting to a cold politeness as she invited him inside. 'I'll just feed the dogs first, if you don't mind,' she said, and was already started before he could have replied. He didn't; merely opened two bottles of beer and confidently turned on her oven to heat up the take-away pizza in its tinfoil shroud.

He followed Fiona outside, waited until she'd put down the dogs' bowls and run the dogs through their pre-dinner exercises, then handed her a cold beer and returned to watch the preparation of the meal.

When she went back into the house, he silently put half an enormous pizza down in front of her, cracked open another cold beer, and seated himself across the kitchen table from her.

'Eat first, while it's hot,' he interrupted when she tried to instigate the conversation. 'There's no great hurry about this.'

There was! She wanted to have her say and get this infuriating man to hell off her property, but Fraser didn't give her the chance. His own quiet, competent attitude towards the meal made it impossible for Fiona to refuel the fires of her earlier anger, at least until she'd finished eating.

Dare ate tidily, clearly enjoying himself. Fiona—suddenly famished—matched him bite for bite and enjoyed every morsel despite her mood.

'Right,' he said when the entire pizza had disappeared and he'd brought fresh beers from the refrigerator. 'Now let's have it, from the beginning if you don't mind, and please try to keep it down to a dull roar.'

I'll give you a dull roar, Fiona thought, suddenly at a loss for words. Beginning? What really *was* the beginning? She finally had to simply plunge in at the deep end.

'You bought my warehouse,' she began lamely. 'And...and forced me out without any explanation or...or anything.'

'I did?' He asked the question in a calm, gentle voice, and for once there was no gleam of arrogant, chauvinistic delight in those dark, dark eyes.

'Well, of course you did!' She snapped the reply, but got no further.

'I did not! I am involved in a syndicate which bought *that* warehouse, although certainly not from you. Nor did I force you out,' he said, voice soft, still infuriatingly calm. 'To the best of my knowledge, not that I expect you to believe it, the building was bought on a vacant possession basis.'

'Because they wouldn't renew my lease,' Fiona replied solemnly.

'And this is somehow my fault? *My* only involvement in the whole shooting match is that I'm the architect who's going to have to plan the renovations. I wouldn't even be in the syndicate, except that it was cheaper, moneywise, to give me a piece of the action for my services than hire them.'

'And the head of this so-called syndicate is your Latin American girlfriend...but I suppose you can explain that away as well,' Fiona retorted, her voice rising in anger and frustration. Damn him! Everything he said just made so much sense.

'Ah,' he said, and then leaned back into his chair with a smug expression. Not a grin, exactly, but a damned well smug expression. Fiona cringed at seeing it.

But he didn't say anything else, just sat there looking at her, letting his eyes roam across her with a faintly but none the less distinctly possessive look.

'I see, I think,' he said then, very softly. Too softly.

Fiona couldn't reply. He'd given her no real opening, and besides, the conversation was no longer on the same plane as before. Now there was a personal tinge to every word, every gesture. No longer was this an argument about a warehouse and a lease; it was a primal argument like that between a rabbit and a fox, and *she* was the rabbit.

Fraser kept her captive with his dark, so expressive eyes, but he said nothing more for what seemed like hours as he patently assessed and reassessed the situation.

And then, 'Are you narked because you've lost your training facility, or just because you're convinced that I—or Consuelo—had something to do with it?'

'I couldn't care less about . . . about who had what to do with it,' Fiona replied finally, unwilling, unable to get her mouth around *that* woman's name. 'I just think it's unfair, that's all.'

Liar, said her mind. Dare was only slightly more charitable.

'From your point of view, I suppose it is,' he replied. 'But that's no reason to bucket *me* for it, and I have to say I'm not much impressed. I can make quite enough enemies without this kind of thing.' Then, after a pause that lasted a century, 'There's more to all this than you're telling me, little Miss Fiona Boyd, but somehow I don't think this is the right time to expect you to bare your soul. So I guess I'll just have to settle for asking what— exactly—you want from me in all this.'

'I don't want anything,' she replied slowly, leaning hard back in her own chair as Fraser loomed across the table towards her, his huge hands reaching out to grip softly but firmly at her wrists.

'Oh, yes, you do,' he replied, on his feet now and drawing her upward and against him, oblivious to her wide-eyed terror, to the way she strained away from him. 'The problem is, I don't think even *you* know what it is.'

She would have replied, tried to reply, but she couldn't force the words past the union of their lips as his mouth covered hers, capturing her lips in a kiss that was at once tender and harsh, demanding and yet somehow caring.

Fiona struggled, or tried to. It was well-nigh impossible the way he was holding her, unless she reverted to tactics much harsher than she believed might be required.

Fraser didn't seem to notice her struggles. His hands still held her own like warm, unyielding iron bracelets, and his mouth, his kiss, continued to explore her mouth, then her cheeks and the hollows of her neck before returning to her lips.

She didn't respond; she mustn't respond, and she told herself so even as her lips parted and her body began to mould itself against him, even as he lifted her arms around his neck and freed her wrists so that his arms could come down and around her body, so that his fingers could play a vibrant tune down the length of her spine before touching lightly at her buttocks to hold her closer to him.

Mustn't...mustn't...mustn't. Her mind echoed the refrain over and over, but it was a losing battle. Far inside her, so far inside and behind so many self-constructed walls of protection, some inner Fiona struggled out of self-imposed sleep and stretched to the heat of Dare Fraser's ardour like a flower towards the sun.

His hands were everywhere now, touching her body with a slow, soft, gentle movement that brought her closer, that seemed both willing and capable of making her melt into him, of making her will disappear, her inhibitions forgotten.

She sagged in his arms, half her mind screaming at her to run, to flee, to heed the warnings so long posted. He was a man; he couldn't be trusted. He would only hurt her, only betray her. He was a man...

And then his hands were on her upper arms again, this time in a grip that forced her away from him, that tore apart the covenant of their lips, destroying the tenderness of his kisses.

'This is no way to get answers to anything,' he said, voice strangely ragged.

'What... what's wrong?' said a voice that sounded like her own, but which she suddenly, frighteningly, knew was the voice of the Fiona inside her, the Fiona from behind the barricades. And she stiffened, her body suddenly rigid with terror at the realisation of how close she'd let him come.

'Everything,' was the gruff, unexpected reply. 'Just about every damned thing.'

And even as she watched, his eyes changed, switching colour like smoke from a soft darkness to a coal-hard black that reflected only her own gaze, revealing nothing of the thoughts behind those eyes, nothing of the man.

'What have I done to make you so damned distrustful, I wonder?' he whispered then, speaking as much to himself as to her. Fiona didn't reply; it wasn't that kind of question.

Fraser's fingers stretched away from her arms, his body reared to stand tall before her, eliminating any sense of the closeness they'd just shared. Part of her was glad, felt safer; part cried out against this divisiveness.

'Or maybe it isn't me; maybe it's somebody else who's turned you so far off men, made you so damned suspicious.' Again, he wasn't really asking, but musing almost to himself as if Fiona was merely incidental to the thought.

Fraser shook his head, the gesture abrupt, almost angry. Then he stepped back, away from Fiona and her confusion.

'I don't suppose you're going to tell me,' he said harshly. 'Not now, at any rate.' He gave her no chance to answer, didn't seem to expect her to contribute to this part of the conversation at all. 'No, not now, but I suggest you think on it just a bit,' he continued. 'Think *very* hard on it, because for the life of me I can't think why you'd automatically blame me for this warehouse business. Or anything much else, come to think about it. Can you?'

Fiona opened her mouth, closed it again.

How could she answer such a question? This was no time to get into a lengthy discourse about how Fraser's lady-friend had deliberately released that lovesick sheepdog to harass her. She couldn't prove the allegation anyway—not that it needed proving, to Fiona's mind.

And now, his own explanation about the warehouse, the lease, his specific involvement. Fiona still had some feeling that Consuelo Diaz might—must!—have known the problems being caused for her, but could Dare Fraser fairly be charged with the same knowledge? Hardly, and, if he could, what possible motive would he have?

'Well, damn it, woman. There's obviously something that's got you all stirred up. Is it such a secret that I'm never to know? That's hardly fair, after all.'

'I...' She got no further. The only statement she might fairly make would involve her plans to run the training school at home, and until she'd done the complete paperwork Fiona had no intention of revealing the significance of that particular problem.

'I think you ought to go now,' she finally managed to say, the words emerging in a gasp of breathless haste that marked her continued confusion. Part of her did indeed want him to go, wanted him gone and wanted him to stay gone. But another part, long buried but now revelling in the freshness of a new existence, wanted him to stay, wanted to bury itself in his arms again, wanted to feel his kisses, to relish his touch.

'I think you're right, maybe,' he said, but his eyes gave the lie to his words. Once again he was looking at her with an expression all too easy to fathom. It was the age-old look of a man for a woman, and the stir of desire that swirled through his dark eyes like a mist was reflected, Fiona feared, in her own.

She shivered inwardly, admitting and yet denying her own need, her own desire for his touch, for his kisses. And mostly, she knew, for his understanding, his strength.

Again she shivered. After Richard, traitorous, lying, cheating Richard, she had sworn herself never to be under any man's control, never to give anyone the power to use her, to determine her path in life.

A woman without a man is like a fish without a bicycle. The catchy proverb of the women's lib movement floated through her mind unbidden, causing Fiona to blurt out a tiny and embarrassing giggle.

The giggle turned to laughter, laughter which bordered on hysteria until she looked up to see the astonished look on Dare's face. He was staring down at her as if she'd lost her mind, and his expression of concern was immediately sobering, although there was no logical reason why it should have been.

'I'm sorry,' she said. 'It's just that...' And she told him of her irrelevant thought, although she didn't try to explain it. Dare endured the explanation, one dark eyebrow raised either in disagreement or disbelief.

'It's your theory and you're welcome to it,' he finally said. 'Although how it affects our current problem, I'm damned if I know. So let's get back to the issues at hand. You're out of a place to train, and I gather from what you've said that you've nowhere else to go. So what's the plan, and, since I'm supposedly responsible, how can I help?'

'I only have the last class of this semester to worry about, and I've already arranged to hold it here on

Saturday, presuming the weather's OK,' Fiona replied in a voice so calm she hardly recognised it. How could he switch off so quickly? Her own body still tingled from his brief lovemaking, her lips still burned from his kisses and her whole *being* was totally aware of his presence, yet he was calmly talking business as if it were nine o'clock on a Monday morning.

Then she realised that her own calm approach wasn't so terribly dissimilar, and she had to try and restrain yet another chuckle at her blatant double standard.

The move brought her a quick look of alertness from Fraser, but he didn't comment on it.

'And what about next semester? I can't imagine you giving up just because you've lost this particular building,' he probed. 'Have you got something else lined up, or what?'

'I . . . I'm working on that,' she hedged, still unwilling to get into all the details of her idea about running the school from home.

Dare Fraser wasn't so easily put off. Nor, she quickly discovered, was he as ignorant of her situation as she might have thought.

'Working on it—how? You've probably got damn-all chance of finding another vacant warehouse; if it hadn't been for a long-running zoning dispute you wouldn't have had the one you did. So are you going to put up a training shed here and work from home? It would be logical, provided you can get the people to drive this far.'

Fiona stood silent, riveted to the spot by the accuracy of his guessing, but more so by his pin-pointing of the one factor she hadn't even considered.

'It's...a possibility,' she admitted finally. 'And surely the distance wouldn't be a problem; we're not *that* far from the city.' She thought immediately of two similar dog-training schools she knew of, in the north of the state, which drew a clientele from far greater distances.

'You're forgetting the Hobart mentality,' Dare replied with a rueful smile. 'Or else you just haven't thought it out carefully enough. Don't you know there are people who haven't crossed the bridge since it got knocked down?'

'You're joking,' she replied, then saw by his expression that he wasn't, not at all. Hobart's Tasman Bridge had been partly destroyed when it was struck by a wayward ship in 1975. The resultant disruptions had been largely responsible for the steady growth of the eastern shore as a self-contained and independent community.

Even after the reconstruction of the impressive structure, the growth in Clarence municipality had continued to become the fastest in Tasmania, and Clarence had gained city status in 1988.

But for all that, Fiona realised that Dare's assertions had considerable validity. Still with only three bridges in the metropolitan area, the Derwent River remained a very significant barrier in many parochial minds.

'There might be a few little old ladies in Sandy Bay who think that way, I accept,' she argued, desperate to hide the uncertainty his comment had raised. 'But people who really want to train their dogs wouldn't be so easily put off.'

'The serious ones ... perhaps not,' he replied with a wry grin. 'But what percentage of those I saw tonight would you honestly call "serious"? The dolly-birds with the tarted up Afghans? I'm surprised they're there at all. And the old trout with the poodle?'

Fiona had to chuckle, although his comments didn't require much astuteness. 'That's my business you're maligning,' she replied. 'I prefer to be thankful they take even that much trouble; most people don't, and they're the ones whose dogs end up causing you problems, I might point out.'

'Point taken,' he admitted, and not as grudgingly as she might have expected. 'I suppose any positive attitude is better than none at all, especially if it puts them in a situation where they get some responsible advice.'

The implied compliment took Fiona aback, slightly. For just a moment she didn't know how to reply, or even if she should. Dare took the pause as leave to continue his own line of enquiry.

'So you're going to try it from home?' he continued. 'But you can't run your sort of operation outdoors, except maybe during the summer. So what plans have you got for a building, or is that another thing that's none of my business?'

'It's...' She paused, now half committed through his questioning alone, and no longer sure of herself. Then as suddenly she found herself going and collecting all her plans and proposal details, for some reason instinctively ready to trust him.

His reaction was far from predictable. 'You can put up the sort of building you need for a lot less than this,' he said after a cursory glance through the plans. 'And a better one, too. But it's still going to be hellishly expensive and I honestly do think you're taking a bit of a chance on getting your people here, especially in winter. Still, there's logic in it; you're better paying off your own facility than spending the money on rent.'

He skimmed through the other details of the proposal, most of them arguments she was preparing to use on the council in a bid for development approval.

'You shouldn't have any trouble with the council given this approach,' he said. 'It's good—very good.'

Fiona couldn't see his eyes, and trying to read his voice she found it impossible to tell if he was being sarcastic or complimentary.

'It's no more than the straight, fair-dinkum facts,' she interjected, a bit defensively. 'I'm not trying to pull a fast one or anything.'

Dare's head snapped up and he glared at her angrily. 'For heaven's sake stop being so damned defensive,' he growled. 'I just *do* not know why you have to be like that, but I do know I don't like it.'

Her muttered apology was cut off in midstream. 'And don't apologise either; it doesn't become you and, besides, I don't believe it,' he snarled, and returned to his reading without bothering to look up again.

Fiona didn't know what to do. She was at once thankful for his openness and resentful of his churlish temper. Damn the man for his attitude, she thought, and took the line of least resistance by going to put the coffee on.

Dare continued to examine her plans, only bothering to grunt his acceptance when she put a cup of coffee beside him a moment later. Fiona took her own cup and sat down opposite him, taking the opportunity offered by his concentration to study him.

His long, strong fingers plucked at the various papers as he perused them, laying the discards neatly to one side and handling everything with extreme care. Whatever else, she thought, he was meticulous.

And single-minded about it! After he twice reached absent-mindedly for something to write with, she got up and found a pencil, which she placed in the appropriate spot. The third time he reached, and found the expected pencil, he didn't so much as look up, but sifted back through the papers and started scrawling in notes in a swift, precise hand.

Fiona opened her mouth to object—they were *her* papers, after all—but she shut it again without a sound, without really knowing why.

And when he reached out his empty cup with a soft-spoken, 'More coffee, please?' she accepted the politeness of the request and turned the kettle back on without demur.

This time, at least, he offered more than just a grunt of thanks, and startled her by leaning back to stare first into the coffee-cup and then at her.

'You've set yourself a rather heavy load for the next few years, according to this,' he said, his expression totally serious now. 'Unless you're planning to give up the television work and concentrate solely on this.'

'Not likely,' Fiona replied with a grimace. 'I'd starve to death, for starters. The dog school alone would hardly keep my own dogs fed, just at the moment.'

'You're not going to have much of a social life, either,' he continued as if she hadn't spoken.

'I haven't got much of one now,' she replied, then gasped at the amount that remark revealed.

Fraser didn't appear to notice. He reached down to sift through the draft proposal again, eyes flickering from page to page with studied ease. Then he looked straight at Fiona, his eyes unreadable.

'I've got a proposition for you,' he said. 'I don't want an answer right now, in fact I don't even want you to think about it in terms of yes or no. Just think about it, and try to set aside your man-hating, distrustful ways long enough to give it serious thought.'

And he grinned as Fiona bristled instinctively at the bold criticism, grinned as if to say, 'See, I told you so!'

'I...' She started, then paused, then said, 'All right.' And was surprised to see how his grin widened and his entire attitude relaxed.

He slurped down the remainder of his coffee and was on his feet in a single, lithe movement. 'Good,' he said softly. 'Now consider this! Come by tomorrow, or whenever it's next convenient, and have a look at my shearing shed. I reckon it would do you for a bit, at least long enough to see if having your school this far out is a goer or not. We might have to reorganise things a bit; sure as hell it'll need a clean-out, but it's definitely worth considering.'

Fiona's eyes widened at the enormity of the suggestion, and the sheer unexpectedness and the apparent generosity. Rising to stand in front of him, to at least try and reduce the feeling of inferiority he so easily created by towering over her, she immediately sought to object.

'No. You're to consider it, not make snap decisions,' he admonished, reaching out to place one finger gently against her lips, effectively stilling her. 'Come and look, see if there's any logic in it, and then we'll talk about it.'

And before she could even think to object, he replaced his finger with his lips in a brief kiss, a kiss that was almost impersonal but not quite.

'It's late, little girl, and you've had a busy day,' he said in that soft, smoky voice that had such power to touch her. There was an instant when she could have reached out to him, obeying her body's wish to continue the kiss, to extend it, to build it into something she suddenly wanted more than almost anything.

But the moment passed, helped on by his immediate release of her lips, by his stepping sideways and past her to reach and open the door and walk into the night, throwing behind him the typical country farewell, 'See you on the next trip.'

Fiona could only stand in the doorway, one hand lifted to touch her lips, her entire being suddenly filled with a strange emptiness, a surprising sense of emptiness. Even the thrusting confusion of her dogs round her feet couldn't quite diminish it, and it persisted as she did the dishes and tidied up her kitchen table.

They like him too damned much, she thought, and began to fear that she did, too. It was a sobering thought, and not a comfortable one. Dare Fraser was no man to take lightly.

CHAPTER SEVEN

FIONA slept fitfully after Dare's abrupt departure, her mind incapable of ignoring his instructions to think without making a decision.

She *had* to make a decision, even though it was ludicrous to consider doing so without so much as inspecting his shearing shed's potential.

Presuming it suitable, the advantages were obvious; the disadvantages, unfortunately, were far less easy to determine. She had great problems with the concept of being further beholden to him, yet her financial circumstances dictated that she reason this out on logic, not pure emotion.

The ramifications still rode nightmares in her mind when first the alarm clock, then the sound of riotous dogs told her she'd slept well into the beginning of what had to be a significant day. How significant, she couldn't possibly realise until she'd thrown on a dressing-gown and rushed to see who was at the door.

She half expected it to be Dare Fraser, but as her sleepy mind came alive she realised it couldn't possibly be. The dogs' alarm barks announced a stranger, and when she opened the door it turned out to be a stranger in uniform.

'Miss Boyd? Miss Fiona Boyd?' The policeman was young, perhaps her own age, and his fiery hair and moustache did nothing to add maturity, though she supposed it was meant to.

'Yes,' she replied hesitantly, leaning sideways to peer past him to count the dogs. All there, thank heavens.

He introduced himself, but she didn't catch his name and only glanced at the identification he tendered. But it was clear he expected to be invited inside, so Fiona obliged, curiosity now getting the better of her.

Her dogs were home; her vehicle was safely in the yard. What on earth could he want? she wondered, and mentally added, At this hour of the morning, before she looked at the kitchen clock and realised it was closer to lunch than breakfast.

He accepted her offer of coffee, sat at the table and took out his notebook, but declined to offer any explanation or begin his questions until the kettle had boiled and she could sit down across from him and give her full attention to the situation.

Just as well! If she hadn't been sitting down, Fiona thought, there could have been a nasty accident with the boiling water.

'Trashed?' she finally asked. 'As in vandalised, I suppose you mean?'

His nod was sufficient confirmation; his next question brought her worst fears to life.

'I understand you were there last night, with your, um, dog-training school?'

A mute nod was all she could muster.

'And you would have locked up after yourself?'

'Of course!' Her voice was firm; her certainty far less so. She *had* locked up, hadn't she?

The young policeman's expression was one of neither belief nor disbelief. Whatever doubt might exist was in her mind, she thought. And not entirely without reason.

Because she honestly couldn't remember!

She could remember the hassles of Dare's appearance, the spates of jealousy at her female students' reaction to him, their heated discussion outside the building and his final departure.

But actually, specifically, remember locking the door when *she* finally left? No, damn it, she couldn't! Fiona sat there, staring into her coffee, then up to the silent police constable whose glance had become frighteningly impersonal.

She *must* have locked up, she thought. It would have been habit, if nothing else, after so long, so many regular classes. 'Or would it? For a horrifying instant, she found herself too ready to believe that in the disruption of Dare Fraser's visit she *might* have forgotten.

'You're positive, I gather?' Even more impersonal, now; did he suspect her uncertainty? Or was it just the standard police attitude in such matters? she wondered.

'I . . . just a moment,' she replied, a sudden, terrible thought spearing into existence. She reached out to sort through her handbag, then sighed heavily with relief at finding her keys—including the warehouse key—just where they should be.

'As positive as I can be,' she replied. 'And as you can see, my key is here, so I didn't leave it in the lock or anything like that.'

'No other keys that you know of?' He didn't seem terribly impressed by her disclosure, she thought. Or else he was just putting on his policeman's persona. Fiona had much preferred the politeness of his original approach.

'Not from me,' she hastened to assure him. 'I've no idea, of course, who else the owner might have entrusted with them.'

'Everybody else who was renting the building had already returned their keys before last night, I understand,' the policeman said, then firmed up his lip as if realising he was supposed to be asking questions, not answering them.

'I was planning to return mine this morning,' she said. 'Last night was my final class. How much damage was there?' Fiona asked then, reckoning it was best to have the worst news now.

'About as much as you could do to a building that was empty to start with,' was the reply. 'Broken windows, smashed wall-panelling, broken lights, spray paint all over everything. Pretty much the usual thing.'

The usual thing! Fiona had no experience to guide her in this regard, except for a casual interest in the evening television news which reported such vandalism with—especially now—frightening regularity.

'And ... You're here because ... well, am I being accused of anything?' It was difficult to frame the question properly, because quite obviously she was being suspected of having failed to lock up properly, or something.

'The problem is that there's no sign of forced entry,' the policeman admitted. 'You're not being accused of anything; we're just making enquiries, at this stage.'

'I see.' And she did see—only too well. She wasn't being accused, but if the vandals hadn't broken into the warehouse, then ...

Fiona's jaw dropped. She stared at the policeman without really seeing him, her mind awhirl with nightmares far worse than anything of the night before. If she *hadn't* locked up properly—and considering the disconcerting effect Dare Fraser had created last night, it was only too possible—then she was responsible!

'But ... but surely somebody could have picked the lock, or ... whatever,' she protested lamely. And thought, How stupid! She knew as much about such things as she did about flying jumbo jets, and from the policeman's expression she'd just made that patently obvious.

'Usually vandals aren't that sophisticated,' he replied wearily, as if he'd heard *that* excuse before.

Then he continued his interrogation. Had she noticed anyone hanging about the place? Was she definitely the last one to leave? Were any of her students still around when she left? Was the door especially difficult to close or lock? It went on and on and on.

And each individual answer went into his little notebook with agonising slowness, excruciating exactness. Fiona, whose replies became an endless chain of monosyllables, was increasingly frustrated by it all. She wanted to do something, something positive, like going to see her ex-landlord, or going to see the damage for herself, first-hand!

After what seemed an endless time, she managed just that—she finally finished answering the policeman's questions, saw him out, then flung hurriedly through her morning ablutions and was in the city with plenty of time to spare before she had to be at work.

The time factor, however, was about the only thing going right. Her landlord/ex-landlord was less than pleased to see her, and Fiona could hardly blame him. It was when he began to detail his reasons that she really started to worry.

'There were only three keys—mine and yours and one that I gave the new owners,' he said. 'The new owners who were *supposed* to settle *today*! Now they're starting to jack up about the damage and all, and who knows *when* it'll get sorted out?'

'I'm really sorry,' Fiona said. Wasted sentiment.

'You're *certain* you locked up properly?' he asked for the sixth time, ignoring her condolences. And even when she replied, also for the sixth time, that she was morally certain she had locked up properly, it was only too clear that he didn't believe her.

Which is hardly surprising, she thought. I hardly believe myself! And yet she *did*! She simply couldn't imagine not going through her normal routine of shutting off the lights, locking the door, yanking on the handle to check. She just *couldn't*.

Finally it became obvious there was nothing else she could say or do that would improve the situation in any way. He was at least half convinced of her guilt, and Fiona left feeling that he'd stay that way, regardless of the outcome.

Which worried her, so much that on arriving at work she telephoned her lawyer and dropped the problem in his lap.

'I can't see that you've anything to worry about,' was the reply. 'Nobody can prove that you didn't lock up properly, and you're certainly not responsible for the vandalism itself.'

'But what if I *didn't* lock up right? What if I'm morally responsible for the whole thing?'

'I'm a lawyer, not a moralist,' was the blunt reply. 'If the police come round wanting to lay charges or anything, or if your landlord starts making loud noises about some sort of lawsuit, we'll have another look. But for now I suggest you stop worrying.'

Far easier said than done, she thought as the day slowly passed and her mind kept backtracking to try and pinpoint that exact moment of putting the key in the door, locking up. Workwise, it was a terrible day.

And when she got home, finally, it got worse.

'They've demanded a delay in settlement!' Her landlord's voice was strangling with anger and disbelief, and despite the fact it must have been hours since he'd had that decision, he sounded to Fiona as if he still couldn't believe it.

Worse, he sounded more and more as if he was convinced the whole problem was *her* fault, and nobody else's! She didn't know what to say, and for several minutes could only hang on to the telephone and listen to his ranting and raving.

'Look, I'm sorry,' she said finally, 'but there's just nothing I can do. I'm sure I locked up properly, I've told the police everything I know about this, and your raging at me isn't going to accomplish anything.'

She might as well not have spoken; he just kept on with his tirade. Fiona finally settled it by saying she had to go, and hanging up on him. The fact that she had to do it three times running was far from encouraging.

Nor was the television news team, which she'd asked to keep an eye on the story for her. For them, it wasn't much of a story in any event, and with no police leads and no new information they were no help at all.

As things had worked out, she hadn't been able to find time to personally inspect the damage to the warehouse, but between the police report and the little bit of work done by the various news services she had all too clear an idea of how bad things were. As the constable had told her, except for the mysterious aspect of the undamaged entry door, it appeared no more than typical juvenile vandalism. Fiona had pondered the situation to death throughout the day, but was no wiser.

And by this time, it was too late to fulfil her promise to go and look at Dare Fraser's shearing shed; Fiona didn't fancy trying to inspect the place in the dark, and she tried not to think about the *real* reason for her wish to avoid his property.

It was possible, she thought for a moment, that she could get to the shearing shed and have her inspection without any risk of running into Consuelo Diaz. But it was equally possible she might, and Fiona simply couldn't face that on top of the day she'd already endured.

'It can wait,' she told the dogs as they slept round her feet. 'We'll do that last class here at the weekend and maybe *then* we'll check out the alternatives.' A firm decision at last, she thought, but it did little to ease her worries. She slept no better than the night before, and faced the next day feeling as if she hadn't slept properly for a week. Her work day was horrible, and arriving home to find Dare waiting only added to her sense of frustration.

'I thought this might be getting a bit much for you,' he said without bothering to greet her—or notice that she didn't have any cheery hello of her own. 'You looked bloody awful last night, because of the vandalism, I presume, and tonight was damned little improvement.'

'Well, thank you so much,' Fiona replied tartly. 'You're just full of compliments, aren't you? Now if that's all you've got to contribute, perhaps you'd like to...'

She paused then, wide-eyed at the thought of how close she'd just come to telling him where, and how, to disappear.

She needn't have worried; he only laughed at her discomfiture, although she felt certain he knew exactly the rude phrase that had filled her mouth.

'You really are copping it in big doses, aren't you?' he chuckled. 'OK, I apologise, but it did worry me to see you so... well, so obviously upset by it all.'

Fiona hardly knew how to reply. She had been worried too, sufficiently that she'd checked back through the tapes after both her weather forecasts, but *she* had seen no sign of her being upset. The magic of make-up had covered almost all signs of strain, and her presentation had been, to her own usually objective eye, quite normal and professional.

He might have been reading her mind. 'Hey, don't go all strange about it,' he suddenly said. '*I* noticed, but I doubt if anybody else did. And after all, I was aware of the hassles and I was probably looking for signs of stress. It wasn't all *that* obvious!'

Typical bloody man, she thought. He thought she was concerned with how her audience had seen her, when her *real* concern was the simple fact that he—Dare Fraser—had been able to read her mood so well.

'Of course; I'd forgotten you were involved with that warehouse project,' she lied. 'It must have come as quite a shock to you, having so much damage that the deal might have fallen through because of it.'

Dare's face reflected his surprise at her remark. 'I would have thought most of it was totally irrelevant,' he said with a frown. 'We would have had to rip the guts out of the building anyway, and a few windows are hardly any great expense to replace.'

'That's hardly the point, as far as I'm concerned,' Fiona replied bitterly, then abruptly shut up; it was none of his business, after all.

But Dare was not to be forestalled. 'That's what bothers me,' he said abruptly. 'Why should you be so damned concerned about an act of vandalism that had nothing to do with you? Or is there something involved here that you know about and I don't?'

'Nothing that concerns you,' she replied, turning away rudely. 'So if you don't mind——'

'But I do mind. I know very well you had nothing to do with the vandalism—I was here with you, remember? And I'm sure you're thinking it's all none of my business, but that isn't the point either, because you're upset.'

'Well, of course I'm upset! Everybody seems convinced that I forgot to lock up properly—and half of them seem to think it must have been deliberate. Wouldn't *you* be upset?'

'Not if it wasn't true,' he replied, then as quickly changed his mind. 'No, forget that; yes, I would, and I can certainly see why you are. But surely you know it isn't true and surely you've told "everybody" that?'

'No, I haven't,' she snapped. 'Because I don't know it isn't true. Oh, I know I didn't do it deliberately, of course, but I just can't *remember* locking the door at all.'

Fraser stood in silence for a moment, his eyes locked on to hers, the expression of compassion too obvious to mistake. He shook his head, his wide, mobile mouth twisted into a grimace of distaste, and he shook his head again before he finally spoke.

'That'd be right,' he muttered. 'And you being you, the result is a mammoth guilt trip, all meals and airport transfers included.'

Fiona had looked away, but now she was forced to meet his eyes, and even then wasn't certain if he was being critical or sympathetic or both. Then she looked away again; this wasn't accomplishing anything. Right as he might be about the guilt trip, she didn't really want to dissect her feelings. All she really wanted was to be alone so she could wallow in the guilt and somehow sort it out.

Her idea! But obviously not Dare Fraser's. He turned away and went over to let her dogs out of the kennel.

'You want me to go away, and maybe I should,' he said. 'But I'm not going to, not yet. You need something to take your mind off this crap, so we're going to give this mob a run before tea, and then ... well, then we'll see.'

Fiona's objections were lost in the exuberance of her dogs' welcome, and before she could repeat them Dare had taken her arm and was leading her towards the back paddock, all three dogs forging excitedly ahead.

He kept holding her arm until he was apparently sure she was with them; then he released her and began throwing the dogs' retrieving dummies, laughing at the resultant chaos as all three animals scrambled to be first in the contests.

Fiona found it impossible to be angry with them, and after a few minutes she joined in the activity, and then put Dare to specific tasks, hiding him behind shrubbery to throw doubles and blinds and other specialised retrieves.

By the time the dogs were thoroughly worn out and Dare had declared his throwing arm equally so, Fiona's mood was back much closer to normal and she was able to smile and declare him a 'fit and proper' helper.

'Hardly a description I'd have chosen, but all right,' he said, returning her smile. 'Now let's get this lot back for their tea, and then we can discuss the complications involved in getting *us* fed.'

Fiona shot him a curious glance, then abruptly decided against her instinctive reaction, which was to refuse. She had to admit he'd been right so far; she felt much better.

Once back at the house, Dare sat silently at the kitchen table while Fiona fed the ravenous dogs, then made him a cup of coffee while she took time to shower and change.

He'd declined to be specific about his plans for the rest of the evening, even when she'd insisted it might be nice to know how to dress appropriately.

'Just be comfortable,' he'd said. So she'd started to slip into worn jeans and an old but comfortable sweatshirt, only to have second thoughts.

'This is stupid,' she told her reflection in the mirror, but that reflection, now garbed in a casual but tidy blouse and bright-patterned wrap-around skirt, presented a far more appropriate image, Fiona had to agree, than just comfortable.

When she returned to the kitchen, it was obvious from his carefully assessing gaze that Dare also agreed. He didn't go so far as to whistle, but the look in his eye was enough to start a faint flutter in Fiona's pulse.

She put the dogs away, then joined him in his utility vehicle as they drove the short distance to his homestead. 'We'll give the shearing shed a quick check,' he'd said, and she could hardly disagree under the circumstances. 'And then—with no decisions or anything, you understand—I'll make you the beneficiary, if that's the appropriate word, of my own culinary skills.'

'I can hardly wait,' she replied honestly. 'All that exercise has made me as ravenous as my dogs.'

'Which may be just as well,' was the smiling reply. 'I've just finished a little gadget I want to try, but if it doesn't work properly we may have to resort to making a rum-run to the nearest pub.'

It took only a cursory inspection for Fiona to realise that the shearing shed, while not perfect, would be more than adequate for her classes. It was, if anything, too big, and would be chilly on winter nights, but the non-slip floor was a godsend and the lighting was great.

'I can't find any fault,' she said after a few minutes, only to have Dare press his finger over her lips while using his other hand to emphasise the gesture.

'No discussion; no decisions,' he said firmly. 'Or at least, not now. Now we go try out my super-duper new barbecue gismo and see if it's going to make my fortune.'

'Agreed,' Fiona replied with a smile. 'And I warn you it had better work, because if I don't get something into me pretty soon I think I'll faint from hunger.'

'When you see this little invention, you may faint anyway,' Dare replied, and casually took her arm as they walked to the big house.

There, Fiona refused even a sherry before dinner, knowing she didn't dare put alcohol on a stomach as empty as hers. Dare poured himself a beer, and sat her at the kitchen table while he prepared two huge steaks for cooking and gathered the various ingredients for a salad.

Fiona was allowed only to watch.

'I might make you help with the washing up,' Dare said. 'But only if this goes as planned.'

Once the steaks were ready, he led her into an elegantly fitted lounge-room, a huge space with fittings to match. The furniture was heavy, solid. The high ceilings were typical of the period and the walls were complete with picture rails, and the rails with pictures.

Clearly this was the centre-point of the family home, the hub around which the entire structure had been planned. Fiona couldn't help but be impressed, although she did wonder how Dare could live here all alone.

'I rattle around like a peanut in a shell, if you're thinking what I expect you are,' he remarked astutely. 'And it gets worse. There are rooms I haven't even set foot in since I came back; the place is a veritable rabbit warren.'

'It certainly looks impressive,' was all she could think of to say. No lie, but in reality the enormous house looked like most rural homes of its era—like a sandstone blockhouse from the outside and, well, she hadn't seen that much of the interior. The kitchen, if nothing else, had been modernised quite comfortably while retaining the proper character.

'It's a barn of a place, and absolutely no place for a man alone,' was the irreverent reply. 'I don't expect it's

been a proper family home since my grandfather's day;
I was an only child, and this place needs a dozen of them
to fill it up.'

Seating Fiona in an enormous but marvellously
comfortable sofa, and placing his tray of meat and con-
diments on a handy coffee-table, Dare left the room and
returned a moment later trundling what Fiona could only
verbalise as a mad scientist's tea-trolley.

It was an amazing conglomeration of wheels and
chains and gears and cogs, but the essential framework
appeared to be that of a serving trolley, complete with
castors.

She watched with growing perplexity as Dare trundled
the contraption over to the room's main fireplace and
manoeuvred it into place, spanning the still-glowing coals
of a fire that must have been lit hours before.

Then he fiddled with the chains and tinkered with other
bits and pieces before adding a few small branches to
the fire so that it flared directly under the lowest shelf.

'Right! Five minutes and we'll be watching the most
versatile barbecue known to man,' he said with a broad,
almost boyish grin.

Fiona, who couldn't for the life of her figure out just
how the contraption was supposed to work, could none
the less see that it was *not* the brand-new invention he'd
originally claimed, and she couldn't resist saying so.

He wasn't even decently ashamed, but laughed as he
admitted the lie. 'Caught, and I should have expected
it,' he chuckled. 'No, of course it's not new. It's...hell,
it's damned near as old as you are! I designed it when
I was about twelve, so that'd be right.'

Her face must have revealed her surprise, because he
laughed again and couldn't resist going into a lengthy
explanation—most of which she couldn't understand.
What was clear, however, was the boyish pleasure that

still lived in his entire attitude towards what must have been a complex design project for a twelve-year-old.

And as he described the problems and the various approaches he'd tried, along with various improvements and additions made over the years, she could almost see in his face the boy he must have been—serious, determined, very insular as might be expected in an only child in the country, and extremely innovative and intelligent.

'I was going to patent it, once,' he revealed. 'But in those days every fireplace was so different and the detail work would have made the thing totally uneconomical. Nowadays ... well, it might be possible to come up with a commercial model; most modern open fireplaces are much of a size.'

A moment later, he demonstrated the practicalities of his youthful invention, placing two-inch-thick steaks on the sizzling plate and declaring they'd be cooked no further than medium-rare.

When the meat was placed with salad in front of her, it looked more like a small roast than anything else, but Fiona's appetite wasn't confused. She and Dare sat across from each other, eating in silence as both did justice to the simple but satisfying meal.

Afterwards, it was all too easy to succumb to the warmth of the fire and the combined effects of the earlier exercise and the fullness of the meal. Dare made coffee, served it with tiny glasses of excellent port, and they both sat staring into the flames, together and yet apart, each lost in thoughts neither shared nor needing to be.

Fiona wouldn't have dared to communicate her thoughts; she was surreptitiously watching her host, discovering the various planes and angles of his rugged, handsome features, the changes of expression created by each alteration in the flickering light of the fire.

How difficult it must be, she thought, to rattle round a family home as palatial as this, a home which must be filled with memories, alive with a history now truly significant only to this one man. What a legacy for the children he would eventually have, so much to share, to teach...

The far-off sound of a howling dog failed to free her from her reverie, but when it was repeated and Dare Fraser leapt suddenly to his feet, she too was quickly roused.

Fiona followed as he strode to the front door, his every stride alive with a strange, tense alertness. Together, they stepped out into the star-speckled darkness, listening— but for what?

Fiona found out all too quickly. The night silence was suddenly rent with a howling, and now it wasn't one dog, but several. And mingled with the horrific sound, a bleating of terrorised, panic-stricken sheep.

'Damn!' Dare's voice spat out the curse even as he spun round and reached into the shadowy hallway behind him, turning back to the night with a rifle in one hand and his keys in the other.

'You stay here,' he growled, and was running for his utility vehicle before she could reply.

'Not on your life,' she cried, and was opening the passenger door even as the engine screamed to life and the headlights threw cones of visibility across the yard.

'You won't like this,' he warned, pausing for the instant it took to throw open the kennel where Blue bounced with excitement. The utility vehicle was in motion even as the sheepdog flew into the open tray.

Fiona was forced to hang on for dear life as they sped through one open gate, then across the open paddocks on a route that ignored existing tracks. Dare reached under the dash, driving one-handed despite the apparent dangers of the terrain, and handed Fiona a spotlight.

'Can you work this while I drive?' he asked without looking at her.

'I don't know,' she said. 'I've never done this before.'

'Just stick your arm out of the window and try to cover as much ground as you can,' he muttered. 'And if you see a dog, try and keep the light on him, that's all.'

Easier said than done, she found, especially with the vehicle bounding across the paddock like some demented thing.

Fiona stifled a scream as the utility vehicle flung itself towards a fence-line that was caught momentarily in the bobbling beam of light, but Dare quickly downshifted, then skidded to a halt and darted out and round to her side.

Fingers like steel gripped her wrist, slowly guiding the light across the adjacent paddock. Sheep materialised from the darkness, shadowy shapes that seemed almost ghostly but for the eyes that held and returned the light. She gasped as he continued moving the light, apparently oblivious of the fact Fiona's wrist couldn't turn as far as his own.

'Let go,' he muttered, and lessened his grip only long enough for her to do so. Then the light continued its steady path along the fence-line, pausing occasionally and then moving on.

She heard his grunt even as her eyes picked up the first mark of the invasion, a sheep whose shape was different, a sheep with clumps of wool hanging loosely, distorting its shape. One, then another, then a small group, jammed into a fence corner with terror evident in their jerky, panicky movements.

Dare grunted again, his fingers moving the light slowly now, crossing from the sheep to the adjacent darkness in a careful pattern of short, sweeping movements.

'There.' His voice whispered; his fingers somehow gathered her own to reclaim the handle of the spotlight. 'Just keep it right there,' he instructed, and she obeyed without seeing the reason, at first.

She heard the snick of the rifle being cocked, and in that instant the dog turned and stared straight into the light, eyes flaring only briefly as it turned to run.

The rifle discharged in a series of 'phutt' sounds, hardly audible over the barks of the dog in the back of the truck.

And in the broad cone of the spotlight, one flickering dog shape became two, then three, all streaking for the darkness of the horizon as Fiona tried desperately to keep the light on their fleeing shapes.

Dare fired again, and again, and with Blue for some reason silent now Fiona was conscious of the tinkling sound of the empties rattling down the side of the truck.

She could also hear Dare cursing under his breath as the last dog fled out of sight, and she numbly obeyed his soft-voiced command to turn the light downwards so he could see to ensure the rifle was safely unloaded.

'My eyes must be going in my old age,' he growled then. 'I should have had the lot of them, but they're cunning devils; they won't hold in the light.'

'You...didn't you hit any of them?' She found herself sharing his anger, his feeling of desperation against a foe so difficult to cope with.

'Doubt it,' he replied. 'But we'll find out. I've got to see how much damage the bastards did, although it doesn't look too bad, for once.'

He waved the sheepdog out and scooped up a flash-light before stepping through the fence to where the sheep were.

Fiona followed on her own side of the fence, and reached the corner just as the dog brought in the balance of the flock for his master's inspection.

Dare quickly shunted away those obviously without injury, but there were several, Fiona saw through hor-rified eyes, that would never rejoin their fellows.

Dare's muttered curses were muted by the arrival of another vehicle, and then joined as his farm worker hopped the fence and came over to him.

Fiona couldn't stay; she turned away and retreated to Dare's truck, the evening's dinner now rebelling in her stomach and tears streaming from her eyes. She was huddled in the passenger seat when he finally returned and began the trip back to the homestead in silence.

'You want coffee, or just to go home?' he asked as they arrived back. 'I'm sorry you had to see that; shouldn't really have let you come.'

'I've seen it before,' she replied, 'although never quite so graphically, I must admit. And yes, I think I'd really rather go home if you don't mind. It's late, and...well...'

'Yeah. The tone of the evening's spoiled just a bit, isn't it?' he replied, an edge of bitterness—or was it mockery?—in his voice.

'That's not really true,' Fiona replied. 'It was a lovely meal, and a...a...generous gesture you provided to help me get out of my foul mood. I'm just sorry it had to end as it did.'

'Not half as sorry as that damned red setter if I'd got a decent shot at him,' Dare growled. 'That's the third time I've missed him, but he can't lead a charmed life forever.'

They drove the rest of the way to Fiona's in silence but a sideways glance at the grinding, working muscles at Dare's jaw revealed his continuing anger at the roving dog pack.

When they arrived to find Fiona's own three still safe in their kennel, she breathed an unnecessary sigh of relief that they couldn't even be *accused* of involvement in the raid.

Dare's mood also seemed to change slightly as they arrived in the driveway. The tension was less obvious, the anger blunted.

'I'm sorry you had to be involved in that,' he said, just after turning off the engine. 'It's never pretty, and I know that with your feelings about dogs it must seem pretty awful to see somebody shooting at them like that, but——'

'You don't have to apologise for anything,' she said, reaching out to place her fingers on his muscular forearm. 'I also know that *you* didn't enjoy it; you like dogs as much as I do, I think.'

She could feel the tension drain away under her fingers as he sighed and then replied, 'I do—that's the hard part. If I could shoot the bloody owners of these roving menaces, I would, although of course it isn't possible. It isn't the dogs' fault, but they're the ones who cop it, even on the rare occasions we can track them home.'

He lit a cigarette and sat silent for a moment, staring out of the windscreen at the looming shape of Fiona's cottage against the night sky. And when he did speak, it was to change the subject abruptly and totally.

'Your house holds ghosts for me; did you know that?' he asked without preamble. Fiona had no answer, and in any event was given no time to voice one.

'I grew up convinced the original Miss Boyd was having it off with my old man,' he mused, almost speaking to himself, she thought. 'I hated him for that; it was one of the main reasons I didn't come back after university. And in a way, I think now because my mother conditioned me to think so, I always had the feeling he'd given away part of my heritage here.'

'Perhaps he did,' Fiona replied, careful to keep her voice and tone neutral. Dare may have heard, or may not have. He continued speaking almost as if she hadn't.

'When I was younger, and most of the time while I was in South America, the heritage aspect didn't really matter much to me, as such,' he said. 'I was aware, of course, that some day I would inherit the family property, but it wasn't a *real* thing, if you know what I mean. It wasn't until the parents died that I suddenly realised just how much of a responsibility was involved here.'

'Not *here*,' she corrected without thinking. '*Here* is mine, remember.' And thought, Mine? It would be all too easy to think otherwise, but she dared not ... would not!

'Yours,' he replied, but it wasn't an admission, much less an acceptance. He wasn't, Fiona sensed, really speaking to her at all; he was lost in thoughts that were somehow being vocalised, but she wasn't at all sure he realised it.

'I hated her,' he said, and she didn't need a map to realise he was speaking about her home's former owner, the original Miss Boyd. 'My mother hated her and so did I.' But now his own hate sounded less certain and his next statement confirmed that.

'Of course, I was younger then. Now ... well, now I sort of wonder,' he said, and by leaning forward slightly Fiona could see the fixed, vacant aura of his stare.

She wasn't sure he even realised she was there with him, was even less sure if she wanted him to. This, she thought, was far too personal, far too intimate a situation. She didn't *want* to be here, didn't want to be privy to such a soul-searching. It would put conditions, restrictions, even chains upon their relationship, and she didn't want that, wouldn't have it.

Neighbours, fine. But she didn't dare let herself become any more involved with this man, not with his ghosts and his memories and his autocratic way of stepping in to control and manage her life. His fixation about her property—*her* property—frightened her. His openness frightened her even more.

I may have to hate him, she thought, and how can you hate a man who's shown you his soul?

Then she shook herself mentally. This was getting quite out of hand, she thought. It was the middle of the night; she'd had a long and arduous day and tomorrow would likely be worse, not better.

'I'd better be going in,' she said, then repeated it, louder this time, when he didn't appear to hear.

'Yes, yes, I guess you'd better,' he finally replied, turning to look at her with eyes that made her wonder if he'd just realised she was there at all.

'You've had a hell of a day, and not much better a night,' he added. 'I hope it doesn't give you nightmares or anything.'

'So do I,' Fiona replied, and pushed open the passenger door of the utility vehicle. As she did so, Dare took her free hand in his own sinewy fingers and lifted it to his lips, his eyes capturing Fiona's as he did so.

She tensed inwardly, certain he would pull her towards him, certain he would kiss her, certain she wanted him to but not at all certain why. But he didn't.

'Sleep tight,' he murmured, and watched as she clambered from the vehicle and up to her front porch.

By the time she had the door unlocked, he was gone, leaving her to the company of the dogs and the waning

night and—eventually—the very nightmares he'd worried
about. Nightmares of slavering hounds and fleeing sheep
and gunshots in the dark. They were brief and didn't
come until almost morning.

CHAPTER EIGHT

MORNING brought little improvement, either to Fiona's mood or, indeed, to her circumstances.

She was wakened by the telephone, insistent in strident tones that she must fling off her covers and rush to answer it.

The tones of her ex-landlord were even more strident.

'The whole deal's fallen through, and it's all your fault,' he began, hardly even waiting for her hello. 'All your fault!'

'But——' She got no further. He was in full rage now, had obviously been rehearsing his attack and had every aspect down pat.

'Don't trouble to deny it,' he shrieked. 'You deliberately left the place open and you deliberately arranged with those hoodlums to vandalise it. You did it because I wouldn't renew your lease—you did!'

'Please, you must listen to me,' she pleaded, having to shout into the telephone, her voice high-pitched in a mixture of anger and shock. 'I didn't——'

'You did! You're a spiteful, vindictive little bitch,' he raged. 'But don't think you'll get away with this. I warn you—I'll fix you...I'll get even.'

'But I didn't,' she cried. 'I damned well didn't. I locked up just as I always have.'

'Oh, I can't prove it, of course. You made sure of that.' His voice was smarmy now, reeking with innuendo and hurt feelings. 'But I know. I've got first-hand information. And let me tell you, Miss Boyd, that your reputation is finished. Finished! Do you hear me?

I'll make sure you never rent another premises in Hobart ever again.'

'What do you mean—first-hand information?' Fiona felt a cold shudder through her empty tummy at this insinuation. What could he know? And, perhaps more important, who would have given him this damning information?

'Never you mind,' he replied, voice dripping with the satisfaction that he'd finally got to her, that he had her worried now. 'Just never you mind. It'll come out...it'll all come out in the end, and then you'll see.'

'But I don't see,' she replied, trying to force patience into her tone, trying to stay calm, reasonable. She had to! Dealing with this man, she'd found in the past, was hard enough when he wasn't upset; agitated as he was now, it would be virtually impossible. She *had* to try and calm him down.

'You will see...my very word you will,' was his reply, a reply fairly dripping with venom. 'I have it on very good authority that you deliberately let those hoons wreck my building, and once I get the proof, well...you just wait, my girl, you just wait!'

'Whose authority?' Fiona demanded. 'I want to know; I have a *right* to know. Somebody is lying about me, and I want to know who it is.'

'You'll find out. Just as soon as the police catch those young hooligans and get a confession. Then you'll find out, and so will everybody else. There won't be any question then, and there won't be any advantage batting those innocent eyes and playing innocent, because everybody will know...'

It got worse after that. Much worse. Fiona suddenly realised—and was astonished not to have seen it before— that her ex-landlord's attitude towards her was based not so much on the recent incident of vandalism, but on some deep-seated and obviously long-standing sexual frustration, one she'd never before noticed.

Or just ignored, she thought. Maybe I've been *too* blasé about such things, because it's something I should have noticed; it isn't something that should be part of any kind of business relationship *without* being noticed.

But it was too late for such hindsight now. Already the man's vituperation was bordering on the obscene and Fiona's temper was rising to meet it.

'That's enough!' she finally shrieked into the telephone. 'Enough—do you hear me? You're a dirty-minded, nasty little pervert of a *thing* and I won't listen to this...this *filth* for another instant. And don't you ever...ever phone me again. Not ever!'

There was a marginal satisfaction in slamming down the telephone so hard it *must* have hurt his ears, but really, she thought as she trudged through the routine of making her morning coffee and toast, the satisfaction was only *just* marginal.

Far more significant was the implications of the man's call! Could he have information that would implicate her in the vandalism? He couldn't, Fiona thought. Unless, of course, somebody wanted her implicated, had perhaps arranged the entire thing with exactly that in mind.

'It just doesn't make any sense,' she sighed after relating the morning's happenings to her lawyer later in the day. 'I accept that I might—might!—have forgotten to lock up properly. I don't think that's what happened, but OK, let's say it did. That's still no excuse for his coming out and directly accusing me of being involved in the vandalism itself. Is it?'

John was his usual laconic self, and even as she spoke he was staring out of his office window at the tower clock atop the T&G building over the road. He seemed to have a fascination with that clock, Fiona had often noticed in the past.

'I think I'd better have a talk to him,' John finally said. 'It sounds like he's just overwrought by the deal's falling through, but that's no excuse for outright abuse.'

'What you have to consider, I'm afraid,' Fiona replied with a sigh, 'is that it's all really just an excuse.'

'Which means what? Have you been overdosing on cryptic crossword puzzles or something?'

'It means that he's...well...he's had some fairly personal ideas all this time, and now he's all shirty because I didn't notice,' she muttered. 'I guess he could have handled outright rejection, but being ignored is just too much for him.'

John's laughter did nothing for her mood.

'It isn't damned well funny,' she snapped. 'I can handle being accused of something I didn't do, even if I'm not a hundred per cent sure I didn't do it, but add this bastard's outright maliciousness into the bargain and I'm not at all sure what he might manage.'

'He'll manage nothing,' was the reply. 'The man's known for his ignorance and nobody who matters is going to listen to him. And if he does start mouthing off too much, we'll slap a writ on him; he's got the money to make it worthwhile.'

'That is the absolute *last* thing I want,' Fiona cried. 'I know you lawyers think differently about such things, but mud sticks and I won't have a bar of that sort of thing. I hope that's clear.'

'There could be a juicy settlement in it.'

'No!'

Her day at work wasn't any great improvement, but at least, she thought at the end of it, her ex-landlord hadn't bothered telephoning her *there*.

Nor did he continue his harassment during the remainder of the week, so she assumed he'd been warned off by the threat of legal proceedings. Unfortunately, none of that did anything to improve her memory of the night the warehouse was vandalised, and the fear that she just *might* have been responsible continued to haunt her.

The weekend, thankfully, was a mighty improvement in all regards. Her students all arrived on time for their final lessons, and most expressed delight in the situation of training out of doors with heaps of room and—luckily—splendid weather.

'It would be great to train here like this even in the evenings, at least during summer,' said one of the Afghan owners. 'It's so lovely and quiet.'

Fiona, who would personally have preferred it if this particular handler had announced she'd be training somewhere else...anywhere else...could only nod her agreement.

She had spent the first class in absolute terror that somebody would let a dog go, that the dog would somehow penetrate Dare Fraser's newly improved fencing to the sheep beyond.

It didn't happen, didn't so much as look like happening, but Fiona's nerves stayed on edge throughout the first class. By the second she was better; by the third quite relaxed about the whole thing.

Even the sight of an approaching rider didn't faze her. Until she realised it was *that* woman again.

As the figure of Consuelo Diaz, tarted up to a level of fashion far beyond the circumstances, approached, Fiona's attention swung from the rider to her students and her nerves strained with every pace of the handsome bay horse.

Fiona had specifically chosen to train in a section of her back paddock well removed from the fences of both her neighbours, and had spent most of the morning mowing—three times, because of the height of the grass—a good, workable training area.

Thus, the arrival of Dare's girlfriend at the fence-line was far less provocative than it might have been, but still a problem.

There was nothing, of course, to be done about it; the woman had every right to watch if she chose. So Fiona took what she hoped was the right course—she waved in a neutral fashion and then ignored the other woman, praying silently that Consuelo Diaz would take the hint and go away.

At first, there was no such luck. Consuelo sat her horse hard against the fence, her green eyes venomous as she stared at Fiona, her students, and their dogs.

Ignore her, Fiona told herself, and indeed it wasn't that difficult with the activity she had to supervise. But the overall distraction was still there; the dogs were aware of the horse, which did nothing for their concentration. Fiona was also aware, which did nothing for her own, and the various handlers were mildly confused by it all, from the way their skills were disrupted.

Well, I hope you're bloody satisfied, Fiona snarled mentally when the woman finally, without warning, yanked the horse around and trotted away. None the less, Fiona breathed a sigh of relief that was all too short-lived.

She had barely begun the next exercise when almost every dog swung round, alert as never before—but not to their handlers!

The rumbling of horse's hoofs was muted by the lighter patter of other, smaller feet, and Fiona turned in anger and sudden fright to see a mob of sheep rushing squarely towards the fence and the waiting dogs.

Her curse was lost in the excitement as the quicker handlers grabbed for collars and snapped leads in place. It was the slower ones who caused the problem; before they could hold their charges, the rushing sheep had become an overriding temptation—the remaining three loose dogs were beyond all control.

Even Fiona's shouts were ignored as the three rushed to meet the oncoming flock, a flock whose leaders were already splitting to either side as the fence loomed ahead.

The dogs, too, separated. One, a young and fractious border collie, sprinted to the left in a desperate bid to outflank the separating mob. The two Afghans, with no such herding instincts but only their sight-hound chase mentality from centuries of breeding, took the right branch, easily outpacing the sheep as they charged.

Fiona screamed and ran with no hope of success.

She nearly closed her eyes in desperation as the first dog reached the wire, but then realised with massive relief that the silly damned thing had never learned to jump. With its mate, oblivious to the shrill calling of both owners, the dog was turning against the wire to run parallel, now yodelling with frustration as the sheep turned back into their paddock and away from him.

The border collie was away, however, over the fence as if it didn't exist and around to the far side of the sheep in a bid to force them into a circle, to tighten the mob and gain full control.

Fiona didn't wait. She caught sight of the Afghan handlers and their charges finally coming together as she hurdled the fence and rushed to try and cut off the black and white sheepdog, pleased to see its handler taking the other flank with leash in hand and a determined look of revenge on his face.

And, as quickly as it had begun, it was suddenly over. The sheepdog, subservience a strong part of its heritage, slunk to heel and accepted the leash, though not without a hard stare for the sheep that now moved off with determination for the other side of the paddock.

Fiona had some difficulty now in crossing the fence she'd so easily hurdled going the other way, and had to help the border collie owner in getting his pet across as well.

When the class was finally reassembled and totally under control, Consuelo Diaz was gone from sight.

Out of sight, but certainly not out of mind, Fiona thought as she saw the class safely off the property. That the woman had deliberately driven the sheep towards her class, and would just as deliberately be reporting— and *distorting*—the escapade to Dare Fraser, Fiona didn't doubt for a minute.

Which, she thought, would certainly put paid to any chance of accepting his offer of using his shearing shed. In fact, that offer would certainly be withdrawn once he'd heard the Diaz report on Fiona's ability to control dogs around sheep.

'And I'm not really that sorry, either,' she told herself as she walked round with her own dogs, checking to see if anybody had left rubbish behind. 'It wouldn't have worked out anyway; not with *his* attitudes about dogs and sheep.'

Besides, Fiona thought, she didn't really *want* to run her classes from Dare's shearing shed—she wanted her *own* place, her own school. As a temporary measure, the offer had held some attraction, but she was honest enough to admit that most of it was in the man himself and therefore dangerous.

Dare Fraser was nobody for Fiona to get involved with, she thought. He was too volatile, too unstable, too devious. Especially too devious. She'd had enough of that with Richard...more than enough. Enough for her lifetime and several others, she thought. Besides, she didn't need any man, never mind one who would only hurt her.

She'd almost convinced herself of that when his utility vehicle swung round the corner of the drive and halted for him to unfold his tall frame as the dogs rushed over to welcome him. Fiona didn't rush, didn't even bother with an encouraging smile; she knew what was coming. Knew, and had decided in the instant not to even bother with a defence—Consuelo Diaz would have had time by now to fill his mind with poison, so why bother?

But when his long strides brought him to her, Fraser did not immediately launch into any sort of attack. He merely said, in his usual quiet voice, 'I can't stay but a minute; just stopped to ask how your classes worked out. No great objections to the distance, or finding the place?'

'No,' Fiona replied, perplexed by his calm. Was he testing her? Teasing her? Her defences, totally alert, now started to numb with the strain.

'I did have one problem, though,' she said then, and at once wondered at hearing the words coming from her mouth without having touched base in her brain.

'Oh?' His own reply was courteous, yet not apparently suspicious.

'With the sheep.' She paused, then plunged into an account of the incident that made no mention of Consuelo Diaz's involvement, simply related the dogs' rush, the subsequent actions by all the handlers involved.

'It was only the border collie that got over the fence,' she said in the end. 'And no harm done, really.'

'Except a few terrified sheep,' Dare replied in a calm but somehow accusing tone. 'Not that a bit of a run would hurt them, although it would have been a different story at lambing.'

'It would,' Fiona admitted. 'And I have to admit, I suppose, that it's altered my feelings rather about doing any sort of out-of-doors training here.' True enough, but only because she now realised she could never be certain of training without Consuelo Diaz's using her position to hurt and disrupt. Without Ms Diaz, Fiona was more than confident of her ability to maintain control.

But no sense opening that can of worms now, she thought. To complain about the woman to Dare Fraser was only to court problems she could better do without.

Besides, she found herself thinking, he'd only defend the Diaz woman; he was like that. And then Fiona found herself remembering the times he'd defended *her*, and was twice glad she'd not thought to accuse Consuelo Diaz.

'There'd always be an element of risk, I suppose,' Dare was replying, but Fiona noticed that although he was speaking to her his gaze was less than focused, and his attention, such as it was, seemed to be on her house, not on either her or their conversation.

He's obsessed with the place, she thought. Obsessed to the point where it's damned well worrisome and not very complimentary either. The least he could do when I'm making this admission of guilt is to pay attention.

Even with her thought, Dare shook his head and ran a hand across his brow as if wiping away cobwebs...or memories.

'I can't stay,' he said. And then added, 'If the guy comes back into class, let me know and we'll sort his dog out for him damned quick smart; it's probably only a matter of too much instinct and too little training.'

'It's a matter of potentially good sheepdog going to waste in the city,' Fiona replied bitterly. 'I keep trying to tell people that working dogs have to have *work*, but they won't be told.'

'Put the dog in a small pen with a big ram for a while,' Dare said, almost as if he'd been thinking, not listening to her at all. 'If you judge the time right, the dog's still inclined to work sheep, but he'd damned well keep his distance.'

And again, she realised, he was looking at the house or, if not exactly *looking*, then intent on it, fixated. She felt her temper rising at his divided attention, and realised the situation wasn't improved by her continued fear that he would, somehow, find some way to get her out of her home, to get it for himself.

And then what? she wondered. Burn it down? Make it into a shrine to his black memories? None of it made sense, and she sensed that it might never do so. Dare Fraser was too complex for that.

But now, he was already moving towards his vehicle, and her own attention was divided. Both waved goodbye, absently.

Fiona found herself wondering as he drove away. Why had he made so little of her transgression? Surely his lady-friend had told him, and just as surely had put the worst possible light on the incident? Or had she? Perhaps, Fiona thought, he'd stopped en route home . . . but he hadn't; she was standing there watching the vehicle turn towards the city.

It simply didn't make sense. Even without a coloured tale from the Diaz woman, he should have been furious about the incident. But, of course, without that woman there would have been no incident, although *he* could hardly be expected to know that.

The whole thing bothered Fiona through her short break for a meal, then somehow got lost in the welter of cleaning and other work that followed.

The routine of vacuuming and tidying should have allowed her, she thought, to give careful thought to her future and the problems that now seemed linked to it. But it didn't; she found her mind not concerned about Consuelo Diaz and her capacity for trouble, but on Dare Fraser and his obsession with her house.

'Maybe I *should* just give it away, the whole damned thing,' she muttered into a sinkful of dishes. 'He'd more than likely give me a decent price; I certainly wouldn't lose on it.'

And yet ... she *would* lose, Fiona realised. She'd lose just by giving up. And Dare Fraser would lose too—or at least, she thought, he wouldn't win!

She kept tossing it around in her mind, up and down, back and forth, as she got stuck into the nastier cleaning chores, the loo and the laundry and the bathroom.

And she was still tossing it around when she leaned on the built-in cabinet at the end of the bathtub, stretching to reach the far end, and the side of the cabinet fell off.

Her involuntary squeal of surprise was muted almost immediately when Fiona pushed herself away—heaven alone knew what species of creepy-crawly might emerge—and her eye caught a familiar shape. Cautiously, she forced herself to kneel for a closer look, which changed nothing. It looked like a biscuit tin, and, when she lifted it from its place behind the false panelling, a biscuit tin was what she held.

All thoughts of cleaning disappeared, not least because the cavity from which the tin had come didn't *need* cleaning—it was pristine, as if it had been cleaned only yesterday.

As was the tin itself. The old-fashioned Arnott's design of the rosella with biscuit in claw was shiny, there wasn't the expected rust and the whole thing looked as if it had been made yesterday.

Fiona knew the biscuit company had put out a repro-duction of that period design, but in her heart of hearts she also knew that *this* Arnott's tin was no repro-duction. This one was real, was original, was... important?

Yes, she thought even before she laid the tin aside to wonder at the ingenious way in which the false side had been held to the cabinet by tiny snap gadgets.

They looked like screws from the outside, but inside they were only snaps, similar, she realised, to those which held the door panels in her old station-wagon.

Interesting, she thought. Interesting, and certainly ingenious, but nowhere near as interesting as the biscuit tin itself. Fiona replaced the panel, picked up the tin, and—leaving her cleaning materials where they lay—ad-journed to the kitchen with her curiosity bubbling.

She put the biscuit tin carefully in the centre of the kitchen table, then prowled around it, torn between the desire to rip off the top and gain instant gratification—or disappointment, since it didn't seem heavy enough to have much of anything inside—and an equally strong reticence.

Clearly the tin had belonged to the original Miss Boyd; Fiona *knew* that without even considering a possible earlier tenant or owner. Equally, she knew without much forethought that whatever it contained was very per-sonal, very private.

'I wouldn't want somebody I didn't know opening this if it were mine, even after I died,' she mused, knowing it was idle talk, knowing she would open the tin, *had* to open the tin. Eventually.

But not yet. First, she had to stare at it, analyse every possibility of what the contents might be. A will? She very desperately hoped not; that could throw everything into chaos. Her heart literally trembled at the thought of what problems a will might cause, despite her legal purchase of the property. What if it had been *willed* to Dare Fraser?

That thought didn't bear continuance. Fiona tried to thrust it into oblivion by shaking her head and walking to the refrigerator, where she poured a liberal glass of Riesling over ice.

Love-letters? That was a far more welcome possibility, although one with problems of its own, since she wasn't sure she wanted to read such a find—and was more sure she wouldn't be able *not* to.

She returned to sit beside the table, her chin resting on one hand as she sipped idly at the wine and stared pensively at the treasure-house of surprises that awaited.

Maybe, she thought with a shudder, it wouldn't be treasure-house at all. Perhaps the tin contained something she wouldn't want to know about.

Another sip. Then she reached gingerly for the tin and, with equal caution, shook it. Then again, just to be certain.

'Well, there's something inside you,' she said aloud to the silent tin with the equally silent rosella—or was it just a parrot? she wondered idly—on the lid. Whatever the bird's species, this one certainly wasn't going to divulge any secrets; if she wanted to know, she'd have to open the tin...and that became a more difficult problem the longer she put it off.

Fiona emptied her glass, went and poured a second one, her attention throughout focused on the moral issue before her. And, she thought, it *was* a moral issue.

'It is to me, anyway,' she muttered without realising she was speaking aloud. 'Damn it, even the dead should be entitled to a little privacy.'

Should be, but wouldn't be. Fiona knew that *somebody* would have to open the tin, would have to investigate what now seemed a mystery, however morally questionable. And quite clearly that somebody would be her! The only alternative would be to take the tin to the old lady's lawyer, presuming she could find him, and *that* would possibly leave her curiosity even further abused.

'A chauvinist would make all sorts of rude remarks about women and curiosity and probably cats as well,' she muttered to herself. 'And I'd have to agree.'

She gave the biscuit tin a final steely glance, then reached out and took it into her fingers, prising at the lid. There was surprisingly little resistance; the tin opened as if it were new, probably more easily.

And inside? Fiona released a long-held breath and laid the lid aside as she stared down at the neatly stacked package of old letters, each in its individual envelope and the bundle tied neatly with a broad ribbon.

Fiona went through the pack slowly, methodically, her mind busy throughout assessing the contents. Most of the letters were addressed to Amanda Boyd, but three were *from* her, addressed to a Sergeant Bill Pierson at an obscure location in Korea. It wasn't until she reached the end that Fiona found the brief official note providing the link.

It was short, poignantly so. It said merely that Sgt Pierson had been killed, and that the enclosed letters were being returned as per his wishes.

Fiona sat in silence for a moment, then poured herself a fresh glass of wine and returned to sit and go through the entire stack of letters, from first to last.

Her first impressions were confusing. The precise handwriting of Amanda Boyd was easy enough to read, but there was an element of what Fiona thought of as Victorianism in the very style of the writing. Perhaps, she thought, it was the preciseness, the obvious deliberate choice of words.

She read slowly, drawn instinctively to the personality that emerged from the writing; Amanda Boyd had obviously been much as Dare Fraser had described—a woman of great strength and determination, a woman also of great pride and self-confidence.

Her soldier, quite obviously less formally educated, was also hampered by the strictures of military discipline as it applied to communications, Fiona thought. His handwriting, although legible enough, was far less formal but often extremely cryptic.

She worked her way slowly through the letters, pausing once to refill her glass and often to sit staring into space as she contemplated the significance of what she read.

It took three readings in all, and a lot of checking and rechecking and cross-checking, but in the end Fiona could only wonder at the treasure she'd discovered.

It had been difficult to believe at first, but once she'd put it all together there was no question at all—these letters, historic relics of a foreign war before she had even been thought of, were documentary evidence of so much heartbreak, so much tragedy, so much misunderstanding.

She had to brush away a tear before once again searching out the relevant information and marking each phrase with a very fine pencil line.

Then, working with total concentration, and not a little shame when she compared her scrawling handwriting with that of Amanda Boyd, Fiona struggled to write down in detail her own interpretation of the chain of events.

It took her an hour and several false starts, but when the list was completed it made so much sense, so much very tragic sense, that she could only sit and stare in wonder at how easily grown people could mismanage their own lives and that of a child as well.

Just the thought of Dare Fraser, growing up as he must have with confused emotions about a woman he'd obviously liked yet not been allowed to know, made Fiona want to cry at the total waste of it all.

She looked at the letters, at her own conclusions, and made her decision without undue thought. He had to know; he deserved to know. Picking up the telephone, she began to dial without giving herself a chance to change her mind. It was late, but not all *that* late, she thought. And even if it did mean waking him—her reasons justified it.

She didn't wake him. She didn't even get to speak to him. What she did get, once the phone had rung twice, was, of all things, his answering machine!

Fiona faltered; how could she be expected to leave a message about something so personal? Then, as the pips signalled her to speak, she found herself doing so without time to think.

'I...I have to see you,' she began. 'It's important...I think, to you, anyway. I...oh, this is so stupid—I just *hate* trying to talk to a machine. Forget it...it'll wait until the morning.'

As she rang off, feeling ridiculously stupid about the whole thing, now that she'd made the attempt to put it into words. It *would* wait until morning; it would wait, come to think of it, for years if necessary. It already had!

He probably wouldn't be back until morning anyway, she thought, and then tried to wipe from her mind the possible reasons why. She'd never thought of herself as a jealous person and, besides, she had no claim on Dare Fraser—nor did she want one.

The thought was small consolation as she prepared for bed with the knowledge that she probably wouldn't sleep anyway. And she thought, Damn the man. He was disturbing her sleep, disrupting her entire life—and he wasn't even there!

And then he *was*. Typically, as soon as she'd finally got to sleep, there he was hammering on the door.

CHAPTER NINE

'ARE you all right?'

The concern on Dare's face was unquestionable, and the dark eyes that roved quickly across Fiona's body in its flimsy nightgown were concerned also.

'All right? Of course,' she replied, trying to stifle a yawn. 'Why wouldn't I be?'

'You didn't sound very right on the phone, that's why,' he replied grimly.

'Only because I cannot abide being expected to talk to a machine,' she replied. 'There's something...well...just not right about it.'

'I'll accept that,' Dare replied, 'but they do have their good points. If it weren't for my answering machine, I'd have missed knowing about this important...whatever it is.'

'Which wouldn't have mattered in the least,' Fiona yawned. 'It could have waited until morning; it could have waited a week, for all the difference it would make. I just thought, well, at the moment it seemed very important.'

'But not now?'

'Now? Well, I suppose...'

'Right!' His voice now took on a different, somehow more intimate tone. 'Well, if it's important now, perhaps you wouldn't mind, A, letting me in, and B, putting on something just a bit less distracting.'

Fiona glanced down, then up to meet eyes that were no longer concerned, but instead were frankly appraising as they roved over her figure.

Fiona felt the colour rising to her cheeks as she suddenly realised how revealing her nightgown was, but perversely felt a thrill at being able to attract this man despite being tousled and far from her best.

She stood back and allowed him entry to the kitchen, but didn't speak. Instead, she pointed at the kettle and the jar of instant coffee, then fled to find something more suitable to wear.

She returned, hair combed and the nightgown replaced by jeans and sweatshirt, to find Dare had coffee ready for both of them.

'Is this better?' she asked after he'd looked up at her.

His grin was brief. 'Infinitely worse,' he replied. 'But for the moment I suppose it'll do. No way we'd have any sort of logical conversation with you in that other outfit.'

'I suppose that's a compliment,' Fiona muttered, then looked hurriedly away as she realised she'd spoken aloud.

Dare didn't seem to notice. He sipped at his coffee, looked at her, took another sip, looked again, sighed heavily.

'You look tired,' she heard herself say, and realised she was thinking more about the state of his health than about why he was here.

'Tired of waiting. Are we going to get to this important whatever, or what? Because if not, I have some important things *I'd* like to discuss.'

'Well, go ahead, for goodness' sake.' Fiona suddenly felt any adjournment would be welcome. She knew he had every right to see the Boyd letters, knew he *had* to see them, but that did nothing to ease her nervousness at being involved in something she considered so terribly private.

'Oh, no. This is your party—not mine,' he replied. 'Now let's have it. What's the problem…pregnant…in love…or have you suddenly discovered one of your dogs is a sheep-killer?'

'Don't be stupid,' she replied hotly, impatient now with herself and the easiness with which he could provoke her. She grabbed up the biscuit tin and shoved it across the table at him with the disclaimer, 'I probably shouldn't have looked inside, but then if I hadn't I wouldn't have realised how important it was, would I?'

'I suppose not, but I won't know if you don't give me a chance to read whatever this is, will I?' he replied with forced sarcasm. 'So it's your turn to make the coffee, if you can manage to do it quietly.'

She snorted furiously, her nervousness making her angry and self-defensive, but managed not to reply in words.

Instead, she silently rose, turned on the kettle, made the coffee, served it, found the remains of a loaf of bread, made some toast, served that, made him yet another cup of coffee, then finally had to sit and fidget while he continued to read through the letters, occasionally referring to her synopsis of conclusions.

Dare said nothing except to grunt a vague thanks for the coffee and toast as it arrived, and his silence only served to increase Fiona's nerviness.

But finally the waiting ended; he looked up to lock her gaze with his own and said quietly, softly, 'I can see why you thought this was so important and I thank you for it, but don't you think it's pretty much water under the bridge?'

'Do you?'

He dropped his gaze, shook his head as if to clear away the cobwebs, then looked up again. 'I'd like to think so; after all, we're going back more than thirty years. In fact, the way you've got it worked out, we're going back longer than that.'

Fiona paused, then made her decision. If he didn't think it was important, then *she* certainly did. It was, after all, part of the history of her property.

'I *do* think it's important,' she said sternly. 'It must surely resolve any claim you have to this place. Clearly your father deeded it to Amanda Boyd because he felt guilty about her brother's accident.'

'*Was* guilty; there's not much argument there,' he admitted. Far too freely, she thought, but couldn't say so because he went on.

'The details aren't here in these letters, of course, but it isn't hard to read between the lines. Dad was inexcusably careless, and it was his carelessness that led to Amanda's brother's death. No doubt of it, and from these letters it's obvious she knew it, so Dad must have admitted it to her at some point.

'I have some vague memory that the brother was hard of hearing, so I suspect there was a warning given he didn't—couldn't—hear, or something like that. I suppose we'll never know the details, but I'd bet Amanda did, and that she chose forgiveness over vengeance, which must have been damned hard for her.

'And quite clearly there was nothing romantic between them, either, because there's no doubt where her affections lay... and died. I suppose I'm happy to have that cleared up, although it hasn't bothered me, really, since I was a kid.'

'Well, it certainly must have bothered your mother, because the letters make it fairly clear that suspicion was the reason Amanda Boyd—formerly a firm family friend—was quite literally forbidden your family home.'

Dare once again shook his head, trying to breach the years. 'Probably menopausal, I can say with hindsight. She started to go fairly strange about a lot of things during that period, but of course I was only twelve or thirteen then, and couldn't spell menopause, much less understand it.'

Fiona felt appalled—not for the present, but for the problems of a young teenager under such circumstances. 'I just don't see why your father didn't...' She floundered there, unable to continue, unwilling to force herself into his privacy.

Dare had no such problems. 'You'd have to have known my father,' he replied. 'He was typical of his breed, I suppose, would never admit the problem, much less explain it to somebody my age. Indeed, he may not even have known, but he'd have backed Mum up regardless—and did!'

He continued, 'Which is why I was bundled off to college in Sydney at the first opportunity, although the fact that we never really got along very well may have had as much to do with it; I was bit of a problem when I was young.'

'But you must have been very close to Amanda at one time,' Fiona interjected. 'Didn't *she* ever say anything?'

His grin was faint. 'You've read these letters—what do you think?'

It was an easy admission. 'Point taken,' Fiona said. 'It's certainly clear enough that when the soldier died at Kapyong, her love-life died with him. *That* was what I found so sad, and so surprising, really. It all seemed terribly Victorian to me—I mean, it's the kind of thing you read about from the First World War, or the Crimea, but in the 1950s?'

'Doesn't surprise me at all,' was the unexpectedly confident reply. 'Tasmania's always been a touch isolated, and certainly was then. Terribly conservative at the best of times. Amanda Boyd was a woman of terribly strong principles and convictions. I have no trouble accepting that she'd only ever love once, and for life.'

He paused, then grinned provocatively at Fiona. 'I'd think you'd have no problems understanding that; you're a person of strict principles and firm convictions. In fact, I rather think Amanda would have been pleased to find *you* here instead of most women I could think of. And I certainly agree with her. Well . . . sort of, anyway.'

Fiona couldn't reply. She was too busy fighting tears.

Lost in her contemplation of a dead woman's concepts of right and wrong, she was oblivious to Dare's voice until he reached out and took her hand, forcing her attention.

'You really do have a problem with compliments, don't you?' he said with a gentle smile and soft, warm glance.

'I . . . I'm sorry; I only really heard the first part,' she replied. 'I was just thinking, how sad.'

He repeated himself, a statement which brought Fiona back to the present with a rush of caution and confusion.

'You can't mean that,' she finally said. 'You've objected to me from the very beginning and you've made it abundantly clear that you'd do *anything* to get this place back.'

'Not *from* the beginning—*at* the beginning,' he corrected her, although she found it difficult to perceive the difference. Not that he gave her much chance.

'I have since come to reassess my feelings on the subject rather dramatically,' he said. 'And, as you say, these letters sort of sink me on legal or moral grounds anyway—not that it matters.'

'It does to me,' she replied, not arguing, just cautious.

'Fair enough.' His smile was still there, his eyes still soft, his whole *being* relaxed, almost confident. 'We both know that, anyway. About the only way I'd get my hands on this place now would be to marry you, I suppose, which wouldn't be the best of solutions for either of us.'

Fiona's heart thundered; her eyes widened.

Dare's grin only widened. 'I wouldn't marry you for the land, and you wouldn't let me anyway,' he continued, holding her with his eyes, forcing her to silence, forcing her to listen, to concentrate. He still seemed totally relaxed, but his grip on her fingers, she fancied, trembled.

'But I really *would* like to marry you,' he said, and his voice seemed to thunder into her ears despite the softness of it. 'Because you're everything I've ever imagined in a wife, and because,' he sighed, 'I suppose I'll have to admit it—I'm hopelessly in love with you.'

Fiona couldn't reply. She couldn't believe what she was hearing, and truly didn't understand it. She simply sat and stared into his eyes, mesmerised, mute.

Dare waited. Did his grip on her fingers *really* tremble more, or did she imagine it? Fiona didn't dare to think about that.

'We could fill that monster house of mine with the children it deserves, and you could keep this for one of them, or just for your dog school, or even sell it, for all I care,' he was saying. 'It isn't *between* us any longer; it's *yours*! Aren't you listening to me?'

She was. But summoning the courage to reply was something else again! She took a deep breath, then another. He just sat there, her eyes gripped by his, her fingers gripped by his.

'I...I can't marry you,' she started. 'You don't even know me, don't know anything about me.'

'I know all I need to know. I know more, I suspect, than you think I do.' And still he was just so damned calm. Fiona, by comparison, felt as if her heart would explode, as if she'd never draw another proper breath. How could she tell him, but then how could she not? If he wanted to marry her, he had at least the right to know, even if her admission changed his mind as she knew it would.

'I'm...I'm not what you think,' she said, gathering her courage. 'I've...been married before!'

And she waited, unable to look away but wanting to, not wanting to see the condemnation, the disgust. He was so typical of country Tasmanians, so conservative, she thought, that her admission would provoke those, at least.

But to her surprise, he only raised one dark eyebrow and shook his head before uttering a bark of laughter. 'When you were too young to know better, and to a cunning, devious, conniving *bastard* who ought to have been drowned at birth. I'm surprised you even gave him kennel space.'

He knew! He'd known all along! That knowledge spun her around, made rational thought impossible. She felt herself yank her fingers from his grip, heard the astonishing words emerge from her own lips.

'*You're* cunning and devious and conniving and...and downright sneaky into the bargain,' she found herself shouting in accusation.

'Only to protect people I care about,' he replied with that incredible calm. 'Or people I love—like you.'

Fiona listened, heard, even understood. But her entire logic was in full flight now, fired by confusion, emotion, and the sheer surprise of it all.

'And what about that...that *woman*?' she raged. 'I suppose you'll just keep *her* around to exercise your horses?' It was, she realised, about the stupidest thing she'd ever said, especially considering the circumstances.

'I'm not keeping her around for anything,' was the calm reply. 'Now look...it seems you don't want to listen to any of this stuff that requires a decision on your part, so how about we change the subject and talk about *my* important revelation? Otherwise we'll be sitting here arguing until breakfast, and there are far more important things to do than that.'

Fiona could only stare as he reached out once more to take her hand, holding her fingers lightly but with a grip that brooked no argument.

'Right, here goes,' he said. 'First off, I've solved the mystery of the warehouse vandalism thing, and of course you locked up, just as always.'

She tried to reply, but was sternly shushed. 'The vandals were deliberately let into the building, specifically to do what they did,' he continued. 'Which was, of course, to scotch the sales deal and implicate you. It took me longer than I like to admit to realise it, but it was easier than I expected to prove, which perhaps makes up for that.'

Fiona stared, silent and now thoroughly confused.

'Now I haven't arranged for charges or anything yet,' she heard him say, 'because I didn't know how you'd feel about that, considering they were only fifteen-year-old kids and they *were* damned well put up to it—paid, in fact.'

'Paid?' These startling revelations were sufficient to pull that single word out of her, then Fiona returned to silently staring at this man who said he wanted to marry her!

She might as well have not spoken; Dare continued his narrative without answering.

'Which means we can't really get to *her*, legally, without involving these poor damned kids, and I'd rather avoid it myself, because there are better ways of sorting out both.'

'Her?' Fiona found herself shaking her head, wondering at how stupid she sounded, but unable to get out more than one word, one idea at a time.

'The kids came from the city's small South American community, so no prizes for guessing who,' he again continued. 'I've got enough influence there to sort out the kids, who aren't bad types—yet. And,' he continued grimly, '*more* than enough influence to sort her out, as well.'

He paused; she stayed silent; he continued, 'I've already talked to your former landlord, who's also agreed to let you have the final decision. He's already got the insurance money, so he doesn't care one way or the other. And,' Dare grinned slyly, obviously understanding the man, 'he sends his apologies, not that I expect they mean much.'

Then the grin faded, his eyes and whole expression became serious. Before Fiona could think to object, he was on his feet, lifting her and drawing her into his arms so that his lips could seek her mouth and plunder it, his kisses repeating his earlier claim that he loved her, wanted her.

'To hell with warehouses and long-lost letters,' he eventually muttered. 'They're not important and never were. Neither is this place; it's yours and it should be. What I want to know is whether you'll marry me or not.'

But he gave her no chance to answer, perhaps sensing that his power now extended in no neighbourly fashion, had no platonic intent. His lips claimed her own, his touch at her back held her firmly against him, where his manhood touched her with less gentleness but rousing fires within her she'd forgotten existed.

Fiona felt herself responding, felt her anger drain away, driven off by feelings of safety within his arms, by even stronger feelings of a passion growing to meet his needs.

When his fingers touched at her breast, her nipple thrust into his grasp. When his fingers slid beneath her sweatshirt, she wriggled as if to ease their passage.

She relaxed into bliss, accepting his lovemaking, his touch, his kisses. Only when he finally swept her into his arms and began to leave the kitchen did she speak, and then it was only one single word.

'Yes,' she whispered in acceptance of now and of the future. No more was needed; he knew where to go.

It was later, much later, that Fiona found logical speech possible, that she found her mind, now curiously relaxed after their lovemaking, able to filter through all that had happened, all that had been said.

'Can you really fix things with . . . with that woman without involving the children?' she asked, keeping her voice quite soft because his ear was only inches away.

'I can do anything you want me to do . . . well . . . almost anything,' was the reply. 'I'll damned well have the bitch out of Tasmania, at the very least, and out of the country if it comes to that.'

Fiona paused briefly, then, 'Would I sound horribly vindictive if I said I'd like that?'

He laughed, the sound reverberating pleasantly through the bed. 'Hardly at all, compared with the way I feel about it. I don't like people messing with my life . . . or my wife.'

'That has a rather proprietorial ring about it,' Fiona mused, wriggling closer, if that were possible. 'I might have to change my mind if you're going to be one of those husbands who reckons a wife is some new type of chattel.'

'Not in the way you mean,' was the chuckled reply, 'and not as new as you'd imagine, either. But then I've never told you how much you remind me, in some ways, of that first Miss Boyd of this house.'

'You won't be marrying a ghost, or a substitute.' The words held a mild reproof that her body totally denied. As did Dare Fraser.

'I said you *remind* me of her, no more than that,' he said. 'And it's true; you both have, or had, or whatever, that strong sense of belonging here, and similar types of attitudes and principles and that sort of thing. But don't make any more than that out of it, although I do suppose it reflects her early influence on me.'

Fiona, unable to bother with any pretence of being offended, said, 'They do say every man wants to marry his mother, for whatever sense that makes.'

'Most men do, I suppose,' he replied. 'But I suspect Miss Boyd had a stronger influence on me, because she was such a strong personality. She was the original and she stayed just as *she* wanted to be, regardless of what anybody thought. Those letters, for instance, reveal a tremendous loyalty to a family that wronged her seriously at least twice in her life, but by her terms that loyalty was right and proper.'

Fiona sighed, but it was a comfortable sigh, one that reflected the pleasantness of her situation. She reached out absently to touch him, to run her fingers along the strong muscles, and wondered vaguely at how quickly and completely they felt comfortable together.

'And I get to keep my land?' she asked, the question rhetoric, the answer an assurance hardly needed.

'For our children, unless you want to do something else with it,' he replied. 'I still reckon you could make it into a first-rate dog school, presuming as I do that you'll want to build that into something.'

'And to get me out of your shearing shed,' she teased. 'And to keep my horrible dogs away from your sheep.'

'Your dogs aren't horrible; I quite like them. It's your other people's dogs that I have mild concerns about. Still,

I reckon we can work something out.' And he rolled over to alter her touch, to guide it, now.

It wasn't until some time later that he asked, quite unexpectedly, if she had any preferences regarding the so-called best man.

'Well, that's your affair, surely,' she replied, rather surprised at the question, considering the circumstances.

She was even more surprised at his reply!

'OK. I reckon John would be a good choice; he likes you.'

'John?' She tried to think, found it extremely difficult with his hands doing that. 'John who?'

'Our lawyer,' he replied, pausing only long enough to reply before resuming his tongue's assault on her breasts.

'*Our* lawyer? I didn't even know you knew him.' And she found herself rearing back, fending him off, forcing him to meet her eyes.

'Stop over-reacting; he didn't reveal any confidences or anything. And of course I *know* him; I went to school with him, for goodness' sake.'

And he laughed at her forced glare of outrage. 'I've told you I don't know how many times—Tasmania's just a big country town.'

'And everybody who's anybody knows everybody else who's anybody,' she finished for him. 'Well, then, you'd best tell me all about you and that...that woman, because after we're married, then *I'll* be somebody who's anybody, and I'll find out anyway.'

'A little more than just an acquaintance,' he admitted. 'I knew her when I was in Argentina, where I was given to understand she was a Chilean refugee. I've since found out that *that* wasn't true, along with a fair few other things in her past, but none of that's especially important.

'When she turned up here, we had a sort of a relationship, as you know, and with both of us having South American connections it's not surprising we ended up both involved in the business over your warehouse.'

'And she was responsible for the vandalism? But why?'

Dare grinned. 'That should be obvious even to you. Pure, unadulterated, hot-blooded Latin *jealousy*, of course. I didn't pick it straight out, because of course I didn't have any particular commitment to her and didn't think she had any either, which shows how much I know about women.'

He grinned again. 'Of course, it became rather obvious when she pulled that little droving stunt in the middle of your class——'

'You *saw* that? And you never said a bloody word, you rotter!'

'I had rather more important things in my mind,' he replied with a slow smile. 'Besides, I knew you could manage a few dogs. And even the woman herself, if you'd had to.'

'Your confidence is overwhelming,' Fiona replied softly, snuggling in closer.

'I just wish my cleverness were as good,' he said. 'I should have twigged to what she was on about long ago. I wasn't needed for that warehouse scheme; in fact there never was a real plan. She'd apparently done a bit of research of her own, found out your situation there, and decided to use sleazy business methods to do the dirty on you.'

'All that just from jealousy? It seems hard to believe,' Fiona said.

'Only because you're not a jealous person,' he replied. 'Which is just as well, because I want a wife who's interested in raising hordes of kids and dogs, not hordes of green-eyed monsters, thank you.'

Fiona couldn't help but grin. 'OK,' she said. 'Any more secrets before I make my final decision?'

'You're already committed,' he replied with a mock growl, 'but no, because there are no secrets in Tasmania; everybody who's anybody knows that.'

'Guff! I don't believe it,' she scoffed. 'There are secrets everywhere.'

'I'll prove it,' he said blithely. 'You've asked me fifteen times now if you can keep this property after we're married, right?'

'What does that have to do with anything?' she replied.

Dare Fraser grinned mischievously. 'Only that I'll say here and now—you can keep your kennel licence, too!'

He was still grinning when she hit him with a pillow, and long after that. They both were!

HARLEQUIN
Romance®

Coming Next Month

Available in February wherever paperback books are sold, or through
Harlequin Reader Service:

In the U.S.
901 Fuhrmann Blvd.
P.O. Box 1397
Buffalo, N.Y. 14240-1397

In Canada
P.O. Box 603
Fort Erie, Ontario
L2A 5X3